First Kiss Fireworks

Port Provident Holiday Hearts

Kristen Ethridge

Laurel Lock Publishing

I0619596

Dear Reader

Dear Reader

I'M SO EXCITED TO BRING you another story from Port Provident. This story is deeply personal to me, and I hope you enjoy it.

As you read the story, you'll get to know Cole Vasquez, a young man struggling to come to grips with the impact of a concussion on his life. What you may not know is that Cole's story mirrors my own. Several years ago, the car I was driving was struck by another driver in an intersection. I suffered six concussions, a Traumatic Brain Injury and live daily with Post-Concussive Syndrome. My life—and my writing life—has been turned upside down, but like Cole, I'm determined to try new things and work every day to be the best I can.

This year, I've learned in a big way that God is in the details. I don't know why I was in that intersection at that moment on that day, but God does—and he has a plan for me. I know he promises life and restoration. He is our great healer, and his promises never return unfulfilled. In short, as Dane discovers in First Kiss Fireworks, everything in our lives, both great and small are "God things" and if we choose to stay in faith, we can see great things happen even in the middle of situations we don't understand.

All the best,

Kristen

Chapter One

"SO I HEARD YOU'RE STARTING your summer vacation a little bit early this year."

Mandy McGovern looked up from her desk. She could feel the frown lines etched into her face. Her week had started with back-to-back long, frustrating days.

"A little early? It looks like I'm starting a whole semester early," she said.

Roger Caldwell, the chair of the Education Department at Provident College, leaned against the door jamb of Mandy's office. "Looks like it. So, did they give you any indication at all? Or did they just tell you that the funding was canceled?"

"Well, I mean what else are they really going to say, Roger? I got the feeling from Stavros that the whole thing was kind of embarrassing."

Roger laughed little under his breath. "I'll say. The whole thing's more than just kind of embarrassing. It's totally embarrassing. I mean, having to completely shut the doors to the Institute?"

"Well, they're not completely shutting the doors," Mandy's thoughts on the subject which now defined her life rolled out on an exasperated sigh. "I think they're still going to have basic classes. But all the peripheral programs are getting the ax. It stinks because I really feel like this program was on the cutting edge. We were finally going to be able to do the research that might lead to providing an option to kids who are struggling to focus in the classroom, due to ADHD or autism, and other similar, brain-related disorders. Right now, it so difficult for them to concentrate and the only thing most professionals have to offer are high-powered pharmaceuticals. What if there's a better answer? I believe there is. I've been waiting to be part of this research for almost two years—it's been my passion, my mission. And now because some politicians can't balance their budgets, the funding is revoked and the whole program is shut down. Instead of diving in with one of the world's leading experts in my field for a short summer research sabbatical, now I have to exchange a plane ticket to Europe and figure out where my work and I go from here."

"I know you're disappointed," her boss said. "And I hate to come here and be the bearer of even more bad news, but we have got to figure out what to do with you for this semester."

"What to do with me?" Mandy said. Her eyebrows pushed upward into the furrows that had crisscrossed her forehead since she hung up the phone call with Stavros yesterday afternoon. "What do you mean—*what to do with me*?"

Roger adjusted his glasses on the bridge of his nose. Mandy had studied with Roger as an undergrad, and now had worked with him for several years. She knew the little signs and gestures he began to make when he was uncomfortable with the message he was delivering.

"I mean, the Institute, Mandy. Well, specifically, I mean their program money—that's what was paying you this semester while you were researching with them. Your salary was being reimbursed through this program. No program, no research funds. No research funds, no full salary. And as far as things here at Provident College, you're not on the teaching schedule for the summer semester and it starts in less than a week. If we have to add another section to some class, I'll call you first, but I can't make any guarantees on that."

Mandy stared blankly past Roger, shaking her head slightly. She could feel the motion, powered by disbelief. The back-and-forth twist seemed futile, like laundry dangling in the breeze.

That's exactly what she was now, a college professor dangling in the breeze because of currency instabilities halfway around the world.

"Okay," she said hesitantly, trying to sort her way toward something positive. "You need me here for something, right, Roger?"

"Well," her boss said wryly. "Not for teaching classes. Are you still going to be able to do any of your research?"

"I don't think so," Mandy said. The weight of realization started to stack brick-by-brick on her shoulders, pushing them down. She felt the heaviness so strongly that it caused the breath in her chest to squeeze tightly. "When I talked to Stavros, it sounded like the whole thing is shut down, permanently. He's no longer researching the protocol, therefore I can't assist him. What am I going to do, Roger? I can't just take some kind of unpaid sabbatical. It's not like I've got unlimited funds in my bank so I can go down to Gulfview Boulevard and play on the beach for a few months of extended time off with nothing to do."

Mandy swallowed, tasting a bitter tang of worry. Her mouth filled with something like the sharp alkaline flavor of magnesium powder. She hated coming across as desperate to someone who'd mentored her for almost her entire academic career, but she couldn't get away from the reality of no real paycheck, so to speak, coming in for a few months.

And it wasn't just being able to pay the bills. Not being able to do this research could very well push her off the tenure-track she'd worked so hard to get on.

"Let me talk to Marty. We'll see what we can do," Roger said, referencing the Dean of the College of Arts and Sciences. "We're low on options and time, so don't get your hopes up—but maybe there's something I haven't thought of."

Another harsh breath forced past Mandy's lips before she spoke. "Don't worry, Roger. I'm not sure my hopes could get any lower at this point. You know how when you're wading out at the beach and then all of a sudden, you step off the sandbar and everything's deeper? In the last twenty-four hours, I've lost track of how many sandbars I've stepped off of. I'm just treading water right now."

Roger wrapped up the conversation with a few well-meaning platitudes, but Mandy didn't hear a single one. Her eyes darted around her office, looking at the textbooks and diplomas and mementos that had so far made up her career as an educator teaching the next generation of educators how to make a difference for students with challenges. Slowly, her gaze came to rest on a photo of Mandy and her mother in front of a church in Mexico they'd attended a mission trip for a few summers ago.

The simplicity of the cinderblock building, painted a gentle shade of pale yellow brought back memories of hard work and pushing past boundaries.

Slowly, she took a deep breath and tried to shake off the feeling of drowning.

Mandy locked her eyes on the vision of the little church, wishing she could be there again, surrounded by community and a supportive group focused on achieving goals and supporting others.

But nothing kept away the feelings of being battered by the turn of the tide in her life.

She lowered her head into her hands and pressed her fingertips in the space between her eyebrows, trying to relieve the pressure inside.

"I need a life preserver. God, is there one out there?"

"DR. MCGOVERN?" DANE Vasquez felt like he was meeting someone on a blind date. Only this time, he felt a complete lack of confidence—and that almost never happened when he took someone out. He believed in only a handful of things in this life. His ability to turn a double play when the game was on the line was one. His ability to get a woman to say yes to a second date was another.

There wouldn't be any appetizers or cocktails right now in the faculty and staff dining hall at Provident College. Only Dane, a professor he'd never met, and a hope against all hope that this woman had the answers he needed.

"Yes, I'm Mandy McGovern. I'm sorry, I don't believe we've met."

"No, I don't think we have. I haven't been here at Provident College very long." Dane wanted to stick his hand out in the time-honored gesture of greeting, but there was no denying his palms were slick with more than a little trepidation. "I'm the head coach for the Provident College Tidal Waves baseball team."

"Oh, baseball. That explains it. I'm usually on this side of campus. How can I help you, coach?"

Dane gestured to the seat across the table from her. "Is it okay if I sit for just a minute?"

She pointed at the empty space. "Sure. I was just grabbing a quick bite by myself today."

"I'm sure you're busy with trying to get your last-minute details in order with the semester about to start. I eat quick lunches in crazy places while the season's going on." The color of her eyes changed from topaz to a dark golden velvet. Briefly, his mind wondered what the change indicated. But, he didn't have time to indulge that rabbit trail. He needed to ask her his question. "I need some help, and I think you might have the right background for it."

"Well, if it's baseball-related, you're probably looking for my brother." Her mouth twisted up a little at the corner, revealing a shallow dimple. "But you said this *wasn't* about baseball, Coach. So how can I help?" She lifted the glass of iced tea in front of her and took a sip.

"I understand you're a specialist in the area of students and brains and focus and concentration and things like that."

She placed the glass back on the white coaster. "Something like that. My CV has some fancier language, but yes, that's basically my area of focus. I teach the next generation of educators how to best work with children who have barriers to focus and behavior, like ADHD or autism or other conditions. I assume the individual members of your team are connected with the resources available to them at the Academic and Athletic Success Center, if they need some help, right?"

"Yeah, the guys do all their study hall hours and those who are eligible for tutoring get it. My request isn't for the whole team. It's for one guy."

Dane had been in a lot of big moments, big games. He'd had a lot of eyes watching him. He'd made the final out and preserved a win for his team more times than he could count. He wasn't used to being nervous. As long as his cleats were on, Dane usually felt like there wasn't anything he couldn't do.

But today he was here, in the dining hall, in front of Professor McGovern. He didn't have his cleats or any of his other good-luck charms to appease any of the superstitions baseball players were known for having.

All he had was his heart. And it was beating so erratically he thought that he might pass out. But Cole needed him. He couldn't give up.

This wasn't a game, but he had to save the situation anyway. For Cole. For all the times Dane hadn't been there.

"What do you mean? Usually all requests go through the Success Center. I'm pretty limited as to what I can do with regard to academic tutoring and such. It's not really my thing."

Dane decided to lay it all out on the table. Either she'd understand, or she'd reject the request. Cole's options were sliding away, like watching sand drop through the neck of an hour glass. It made Dane feel helpless. And that meant he had to settle down his beating heart and ask for what he needed.

He wasn't even against begging, but the woman in front of him with the low ponytail and striped knit blouse seemed way too classy to fall for that trick.

"He doesn't need tutoring. He's tried that. Cole was hit by a pitch last year. It hit him just above the temple. He hasn't passed any of his concussion protocols since then, but I'm not asking for your help to try and get him back on the field. He's just barely keeping up with his classes, but it's not because of the material—he doesn't need tutoring. He said his brain is constantly in a fog and he can't focus on doing his work. He sits down to read or to write a paper and after ten minutes, he is done. He's on to something else. He can't concentrate. The doctors said all they can tell him to do is rest. But if he can't get focused and get his grades up, I'm going to have to take him off scholarship."

"What year is he?" She seemed to be considering his plea.

"He's a freshman. This is his first year at Provident College."

A student worker placed a plate in front of Dr. McGovern. She smiled and told her thank you and said she'd hoped the young woman had spent a good summer at home. The student smiled and said she had, and she was looking forward to starting her student teaching in the fall. It seemed like they knew each other well, and Dane couldn't help but notice the sound of respect in the student's voice.

He needed someone who was sharp, who was respected, on his team for this project. He just needed Mandy McGovern to agree to at least meet Cole. Dane had done his research. There wasn't anyone else on Provident Island who had the skills or the background to give Cole any new hope.

"That's really awesome that you started his scholarship anyway after he was injured before enrolling." She smiled warmly.

"Well, I needed to. I'm his dad."

"Oh, so you're pulling double-duty, Coach Dad."

The phrase got under his skin a bit. He'd never coached Cole in a single game. Dane was both Cole's coach and his dad strictly in name only. "I guess you could say that."

"Well, I'm sure you've been told there's no magic bullet to help someone recover from a Traumatic Brain Injury. TBIs are unique. Everyone tends to respond in their own way. And you're right, most neurologists recommend rest because that's the generally-accepted protocol."

Dane felt his thumping heart fall to his feet. This pursuit had been for nothing.

"So you're saying there are no other options?"

The professor shook her head.

"I'm not saying that at all. There aren't many conventional options. But the brain is a complex organ, and most people who work with it will admit that they only know the tip of the iceberg about what it does and how it works. I certainly feel that way with the research and teaching I do." She tapped her finger on the table resolutely. "In fact, speaking of research, come to my office in Porter Hall in the morning. Bring Cole. Will ten o'clock work for you?"

"We can make it work."

All Cole needed was a chance. Dane would make anything work to prove to his son that this time, his dad was in it for the long haul.

"THANKS FOR PICKING me up. Not sure what's going on with my truck." Dane opened the passenger side door to the yellow truck with red stripes. "I'll call Mike Renwick over at the mechanic's sometime tomorrow. I hope this won't be a major bill. I've got too many bills coming."

"Bills coming?" Dane's cousin Rigo, Chief of the Port Provident Beach Patrol, let out a laugh. "You can see into the future now?"

Dane threw his bag into the back seat of the truck. "I don't need to be some kind of psychic to know that there is going to be a cost associated with the medical treatments Cole needs to get well."

Rigo pulled the truck out of the parking lot and began to leave the large lights over the ballpark in the distance. "I'm sorry, *Primo*. I didn't mean to make light of it. I didn't know that's what you were talking about."

"It's okay. You didn't know." Dane glanced down at his cell phone, checking the time. "I owe Cole's mom a call about last week's medical appointments. She knows I'm working hard to uncover something new that Cole didn't have access to back home, but I hate calling her and giving her another update that's nothing but dead ends. But I may have a better status report next week."

"Really? What's going on?" Rigo slowed down and pulled into a parallel parking spot along Gulfview Boulevard. Once stopped, he pointed a finger out at two surfers paddling out to open water. "I think there's a rip current out there. Look how the waves are breaking. See that flat area around the rock jetty? The whole island has been under a red flag all day, which means no swimming—but of course, some people just can't help themselves and go anyway, endangering themselves and others. I need to keep an eye on these guys for a second—my lifeguard crews just went in for the day about fifteen minutes ago—but you keep talking. I can listen while I watch."

Dane looked at the waves rolling in. A current snaking out toward the horizon clearly confirmed Rigo's suspicions.

"I met someone today—she teaches at PC in the school of education, and her specialty is helping teachers prepare to work with students who need adaptations in the classroom, much like Cole does now."

"I didn't know that was even a thing."

"It is. I've had guys on the team who got specialized assistance from our Success Center. But I'm not sure if I want to get hopeful about what she could do for Cole. I don't want to let him down again—and I don't want to let myself down, either." Frustration crowded into Dane's soul. He could feel it rubbing out the hope he'd had earlier today, just as effectively as if he had sandpaper running through his veins. What if pursuing this crazy idea was a waste of time? What if he was swimming under a red flag, so to speak? "Maybe it's best that I don't even tell Cole about meeting her until I get some more details."

"So, you think something like that—wait. We have to go. Now. He's being pulled out too far."

In lightning-quick seconds, Rigo jumped out of the truck, grabbed an orange rescue device from the bed. He yanked a radio from his belt and tossed it at Dane. "Call for backup now. Tell them where we are and that there's a surfer struggling with a rip current."

With that, Rigo took off running for the stairs that led down to the beach. He kicked his shoes off as he hit the sand, and never faltered in stride.

Dane followed behind him as fast as he could, adrenaline surging through every fiber of his body. Rigo had been exactly right to pull over. Even while they were driving, he saw a little flicker of something out of the ordinary and instinct took over, directing his next steps.

By the time Dane reached the shoreline—talking with Beach Patrol dispatch as he ran—Rigo had already made it out waist deep, then he began to swim with smooth, clear strokes, edging outside the current, and swimming counter to the direction of the dangerous water.

In just minutes, Rigo had caught up to the endangered swimmer, and tossed the orange rescue can to the man. Seconds later, two other lifeguards jumped out of a truck and charged straight into the water, meeting Rigo and the victim as they came back on shore.

Each lifeguard had a role to play, supporting the tired young man as he got back on dry sand. A third lifeguard ran over to the man's friend, who had not gotten caught in the stream. He had managed to get back to shore unassisted, but the woman in the red swimsuit put her arm around his shoulders and walked slowly in lockstep with him, guiding him to the truck to meet up with his friend.

Dane tried to stay out of the way. But as he did so, he continued to survey all the effort still taking place to stabilize the wayward surfer and the situation he'd found himself in.

"He's going to be okay," Rigo said a few moments later, placing a still-damp hand on Dane's shoulder.

"Thanks to you," Dane said, turning to look at the last whispers of the sunset, streaking low against the edge where the water met the sky. "You knew what to look for and what to do."

Dane let out a rough sigh without even realizing he'd been holding the breath.

"What's on your mind?"

The cousins stood parallel to each other and silence slipped across the beach as the Beach Patrol trucks pulled away.

"Cole."

"He's going to be okay, too, Dane." Rigo spoke with certainty in his voice.

"I wish there was someone like you for him. Someone who could see the signs, jump into action, and know exactly what to do."

"I remember the black of the night when Hurricane Hope washed through the island. I remember not thinking much about what was to come...until I got the call from Gloria that she needed me. She didn't want to call me. But I was her last chance." Rigo crossed his arms across his chest, thoughtful for a minute. "Maybe you've already met your miracle. A hurricane called Hope taught me a lot about not giving up and not believing in mere coincidence. Maybe you met this professor for a reason. And maybe you needed to join me tonight for a reminder not to give up."

Chapter Two

MANDY COULDN'T GET her fingers on the keyboard to her computer fast enough when she returned to her office after lunch. From the minute the baseball coach walked away from the table, her mind had started swimming.

Such was the life of a college professor who loved to research. Once an idea sparked in her mind, she had to answer the curiosity.

She began clicking through files and pulling up her notes, trying to see if the ideas that Stavros had for cognitive improvement in children could also have the same effect on concussion patients. As she scanned through file after file, Mandy began to think that maybe it was possible. Turning to the Internet, Mandy opened her browser and began searching even more deeply.

Three hours later, the sound of footsteps in the hall distracted her from reading the fine print of yet another medical study. She looked over at the clock and realized she'd been immersed in the search for knowledge for the better part of the afternoon.

All the signs she'd seen this afternoon pointed in one clear direction. One question remained in her head: *what if?*

What if her research wasn't going to end, as she'd thought. *What if* it was just beginning? *What if* she didn't have to travel halfway around the world to get what she needed to change lives?

Mandy pushed her chair back and almost knocked it to the ground in her excitement. She left the office, closed the door firmly behind her and headed down the hall to where Roger worked.

"Is he in? I need to talk to him."

Mandy wasn't usually a woman of few words, and she genuinely liked the department secretary, Mary Scott. But she didn't have time for the inevitable questions Mary would have about Mandy's change in travel plans.

There would be time to sort all that out later, but for one Cole Vasquez, every minute counted.

"I think he's finishing up last minute changes the syllabus for the curriculum management course. I still need to get those printed out in order to have them ready for his first class."

"Okay," Mandy agreed, willing to say just about anything in order to get in front of Roger to talk through everything that was in her mind at this moment. "I promise I won't take long."

Mandy knocked on the door with three sharp raps.

"Come on in."

When she opened the door, the chair of the department was indeed where his assistant said he would be, sitting behind the desk chewing on a pencil and staring down his computer monitor.

"Roger, what if I didn't have to go to Greece?" Her heart pounded a little as she threw the *what if* out to her boss.

"Mandy, you're not going to Europe," he stated matter-of-factly.

"I know. But what if it didn't matter?"

"I'm not following you. Did you have a conversation with Stavros?"

Mandy shook her head. "No, no not with Stavros. Do you know Dane Vasquez, the baseball coach?"

"I've heard the name." Roger hesitated slightly. "I think I met him at some luncheon last year right after he came on board. But I don't get out to many baseball games. It's not really my thing."

"Understood." Mandy nodded. "But did you know that his son plays on the team? Well, actually he doesn't play right now."

"No, I wasn't aware that his son was here too. But what do you mean he plays, but doesn't play?" Roger leaned forward, still chewing on the wooden center of the yellow pencil.

"His son was recruited to come here and play for Dad. But he was hit by a pitch his senior year of high school. He's still suffering the effects of the TBI. He's probably got post-concussive syndrome and maybe who knows what else. Anyway, he hasn't been cleared to play since he got here. And now, his grades are suffering and he's probably going to lose his scholarship if he can't bring them back up. Coach Vasquez stopped me today and said he'd heard about some of the work I do with ADHD kids and was wondering if there was anything I could do to help Cole with his inability to focus now due to the concussion."

"Okay, I see where you're going. I think. Keep talking." Roger leaned back in his chair and tucked the well-chewed pencil behind his ear.

"I think the work I wanted to do this summer might could instead happen here. Stavros's lab is gone, but what if we had a lab at Provident College?"

Roger's chair jerked forward and he waved his hands. "Whoa. Whoa. Whoa. I don't even have budget to pay you this semester. I certainly don't have the money to set up a lab for experimental therapies, no matter how good of an idea you think it is."

Mandy paced across the room, trying to gather her thoughts. She knew she'd get one shot to get Roger on her side. She had to convey the most important details to him and not let her emotions take over her request.

"I know that, Roger. I'm not asking for it right now. But, if I could do the do the work—see if it holds up—I've found so much background and other studies online in PubMed and some other places today regarding this same idea in concussion patients. What if I started with Cole, tested some ideas and then if it looks successful, maybe I could put together a full workup to pursue grant funding to build the lab here. We could be a leader in this. You know it was worth my going halfway around the world this semester because nobody else is testing these kinds of things in real time—especially not as they apply to kids. Let me work with Cole, see if it's worthwhile. Then we can go from there."

"You don't have any teaching responsibilities, Mandy, so you can work with whoever you want to work with."

"I was hoping we could find a way to pay me to do it," she said with a lopsided grin. *Just call me Captain Obvious*, she thought as she waited for her boss' thoughts on the matter.

"Maybe the coach can pay you. It's his kid, after all." Roger's advice was practical—but not entirely probable. "I don't have it in the budget, he's got to fund it. I'll support you in any way I can, Mandy. I'll give you whatever air cover I can. I'll support any research that comes out of it. I'll support any grant proposal you pull out of it. If you're able to get a lab here, I'll support setting it up and bringing Stavros from the other side of the world to Port Provident. But you've got to find the funding elsewhere. I just don't have it. I wish I did, but I don't."

Mandy swallowed hard. Her left hand reached up and toyed with the end of her ponytail.

"Okay. You don't have any ideas for funding?"

"Not a one," said Roger. "But the athletics department budget seems to have a certain...um, cushion...in it every year. Maybe you could meet with Peter Downley, he's the Athletic Director. Maybe he's got an idea."

She'd never actually met the AD. She couldn't just barge in there and ask him to put her on the payroll. "Maybe so, Roger, maybe so. But you'll support me if I do this?"

"One hundred percent." He took the pencil from behind his ear and pointed it at her.

She had her marching orders. Now to figure out the battle plan.

"I THINK SHE'S GOING able to help you, Cole, I really do. I wouldn't be bringing you here if I didn't feel like maybe there was something that the doctors just didn't know—hadn't told us. She does research, she'll know the latest and greatest. And that's what we need. Something new. Something that hasn't been tried before."

Dane walked up the steps to Porter Hall with Cole following about a half-step behind. The younger Vasquez didn't share his father's enthusiasm for this visit.

Well, it wasn't really enthusiasm...it was the sense of something—*anything*. His son needed help. Dane knew he hadn't been around to give help much during the last 18 years, but now he'd made big changes in his life. And his son had made a big sacrifice to come play for the Tidal Waves, to come play once for his real father. Dane had let his son down for most of the boy's life. He had one last chance to change and earn the young man's trust. He wasn't going to throw that away like a wild pitch.

"Dad, I'm just tired of doctors. I'm tired of appointments. I'm tired...I'm just tired, Dad. Just thinking about starting something else makes my head hurt, and these days everything makes my head hurt—but I can't do anything about it. I spend most of my days wanting to sit in a dark room and take a nap while my friends and my teammates are going to do normal college things. I don't even want to join them, and I hate that."

Dane's heart broke to hear the flat tones in the boy's voice. Cole had basically resigned himself to his fate. That this new life with a brain injury would be as good as it would ever get for him. Cole's life as he knew it came to a dead stop when his head collided with a pitch. And sadly, he appeared to have accepted that as his future.

Well, Dane hadn't accepted it. He never would. He was slow to the uptake on this parenting thing, but he did know that parents were supposed to keep fighting for their kids.

"Yeah I know, Son. That's why we're here. If there's someone in Port Provident, or someone in Houston, or someone in Texas who has a better idea than what we've been told by your doctors back home, then we're going to find them. And that search starts here, today, in our own backyard. If she doesn't have anything to offer, we'll move on. Texas is a big state—there's someone here somewhere who can help you. TBI is not going to be a life sentence for you."

He felt the sharp steel-like edge of anger slicing at the words as they rose from his throat. Dane meant every word. Traumatic Brain Injury would not be the story of Cole Vasquez's life.

They took the stairs to the third floor where Mandy McGovern's office was tucked at the end of the long hallway. It was ten o'clock sharp when Dane knocked on the door.

"Come in," a voice from inside the room said brightly.

Dane liked her enthusiasm. He liked Dr. McGovern's willingness to help. And as Dane and his son stepped inside the office, Dane noticed the professor's hair was once again styled in the same long golden ponytail that reminded him a little bit of Rapunzel.

If he was honest, he liked that too.

"Hi, Dr. McGovern." Dane gestured to the young man standing next to him. "This is my son Cole Vasquez. Thanks again for seeing us today. We really appreciate it."

Mandy pointed at the two chairs in front of her desk.

"It's my pleasure. I really hope that I can help—please have a seat. It's nice to meet you, Cole."

In return, Cole offered a brief nod like he was signaling an upcoming pitch to his catcher. "It's nice to meet you too, Dr. McGovern."

Dane heard the hesitation in his son's voice. He knew that even something as laid back as this introductory session could be too much for Cole. Walking over here, sitting in a room with fluorescent lights overhead, keeping up with conversation—they'd discovered that all of those could trigger a "flooding" sensation in Cole's brain and send him straight for a migraine and then to his bed for the rest of the day.

Still, Dane hoped Mandy didn't notice that Cole was holding something back. She was the best chance to make something happen for this semester to get his grades back up. Dane needed to keep Cole in school to give the teenager a shot at being on campus so he could then be a part the game they both loved and wanted to play together. The professor with the swishing ponytail couldn't think they weren't grateful an opportunity like this, to find out if she had any new ideas for them to try.

"So, Cole, your dad tells me that you have some issues lingering from the concussion you got last year. Tell me about what that's like."

Mandy focused her eyes directly on Cole, shutting out all distractions. Dane noticed they were a light shade of hazel, like a tree's leaves gently changing to fall.

"I was hit in the head by a pitch. Just didn't see it coming...just couldn't get out of the way fast enough. It knocked me to the ground. They say I was out for a few minutes. So, the next thing that I remember, my coaches were helping me off the field, then they called an ambulance and sent me straight to the ER. The doctor there did tests but said it was just a concussion, and probably within a couple weeks I'd be back to normal in the field. He said everything would be fine." Cole stopped his stream-of-consciousness recollection and wiped his nose as he gave a sniff. He cleared his throat twice before speaking again. "But it wasn't."

At his son's description, Dane's heart broke like a child snapping a twig. He could almost hear the click inside his chest as it popped in two.

Mandy never looked away. It was clear she was very comfortable talking to students. She seemed like she was in her element—asking questions and getting to know her subject better.

"So tell me, what are the symptoms that you have? Tell me all of them—not just the things that you think pertain to the classroom."

Cole closed his eyes. Dane could tell his son was carefully processing how he wanted to reply. "The worst part is that my head just gives out. I can be going along, doing fine, more or less. Then all of a sudden it just feels like Silly Putty is melting in there, like my brain just says, 'nope, we're done, come back another day'." And I have to go take a nap, or lay down—just get away from wherever I am. Bright lights and too much noise bother me, and so even just being in a classroom with the overhead lighting—or walking across campus and listening to the sounds of the other students talking and yelling as they run by—or even being out there in the middle of the day with the sun shining—it just all sets me off."

Mandy wrote some notes on a scratch pad in front of her, then turned one hundred percent of her focus back to Cole. "Tell me more about when you're in class."

Cole dropped his head. "I just can't even focus. I start off with good intentions, but it feels like before my professors even get into the lesson, I'm lost. I got straight A's in high school, so I don't understand what's going on here. It's just so frustrating and I want it to stop."

The sound of a deep breath filled the room. "I just want to be normal again. I want to be me."

Mandy reached her hand across the desk toward Cole and gave him a reassuring pat. "I know it's frustrating. Did you say you've had concussions before?"

"Yeah a couple. I think everyone who plays sports has 'em, right?"

Finally, a little bit of laughter. Dane clung to the fleeting hope offered by the small chuckle and the connection between his son and the professor.

"It sure seems like it, doesn't it?"

"Man, I just thought it was normal." Dane jumped in. "I mean, I've gotten beaned a bunch of times, and some were worse than others, but I've never felt as bad as Cole feels—or for as long as he's felt this way.

"Well, we know the effects of TBI and Post-Concussive Syndrome are cumulative," Mandy said. Look at the NFL players and the helmet lawsuit—there was even a movie about it not too long ago. The evidence now shows that the more concussions you have, the longer it will take you to get better. And while I'm certainly not a specialist in this area, I do know from some work I've done that the brain is fluid, and so if you get hit on one side there's a good chance that your brain moves and hits on the other side—or up or down and so you may wind up with multiple concussions from the same incident, or even something else. But diagnosing so many things in our brains is hit-or-miss because we can't see. Doctors and others like me have to use our best guess about what's going on. So, have you visited a neurologist?"

"Yeah, my mom took me to one in Illinois. He just said to rest." Cole gave another laugh, but this one was tinged with the bitter frost of sarcasm. "And that's about all I can do these days. I mean, do you know how embarrassing it is for a college student to go to bed at eight or nine o'clock? That's like grandparent time."

Mandy put down her pen, and a broad smile spread across her face. "Hey now, I resemble that bedtime, and I'm not a grandparent. I may be a crazy cat lady, but I'm not a grandparent."

"Well it's probably not as big of a deal to you, I guess, if you're not trying to get someone to go on a date or something."

Dane hadn't heard Cole talk about anyone he was interested in dating. His parent radar went up. But then, when Mandy replied, Dane discovered his blonde-with-a-ponytail radar stretched up even higher.

"You've got me there. Not many hot dates for the college professor crazy cat lady."

He hadn't been in Port Provident long, but Dane decided that all the men in this town were nuts if they weren't lining up to ask Mandy McGovern out. She was smart, compassionate, and quite frankly, downright good-looking when she smiled—or when her casual ponytail gave a little swish.

"Okay, grandparent time and crazy cat lady time. Either way, it's not cool. That's when my friends are going out—not going to bed."

"I've taught college students long enough," Mandy said with a laugh. "Explain no more. So, do you have a neurologist you're working with here? Illinois is a long way away."

"I went to go see one in Houston, and he told me the same thing as the first guy. I haven't been back. I don't see what the point is." Cole sounded defeated, like he'd watched his team get run-ruled before being sent to the showers.

"Hmm, okay." Mandy tapped her pen on the edge of the desk. "I think the first thing we need to do is to get you in with a neuropsychologist at Provident Medical Center to do a full neurocognitive exam. After that, we will know better where you stand and what you can do. So I'll take the first action item to make a few phone calls. Hopefully I can find some strings to pull and we can get this done quickly."

Dane nodded his head. "I can get you all his insurance information, and we'll make sure that his schedule works with whatever you come up with."

Mandy's ponytail swished a little again as she nodded affirmatively. "I appreciate that. We know Cole has tried the standard treatment of rest, but he's not getting the results you're both hoping for. If you're both in agreement, I'd like to try a few therapeutic elements from the study I was supposed to be a part of this summer. The study's been cancelled, but if we can find a way to work together, maybe I can see if we were on the right track and maybe get some support to re-open the study, this time here at Provident College."

Everything sounded positive to Dane, except for one thing. He jumped into the conversation. "If we can find a way to work together? What do you mean? I thought you were going to help Cole."

"It's complicated," she said. Her ponytail came to a full stop and a shrewd half-smile spread across Mandy's face. The glare from the lights overhead caught some stray lipstick shimmer left in the middle of her bottom lip.

"How so?" Dane felt like he had whiplash. First they were moving forward, making appointments, discussing options. Now the word *if* had been brought into the conversation. It hit the hope in his heart like the jerk of anti-lock brakes.

"Don't worry, I'm going to find a way to help Cole. But I was supposed to be abroad doing a short research sabbatical this summer. So, I'm actually not on PC's payroll right now. The research team in Europe was supposed to pay me. But now that I'm staying here, I'm not on the schedule to teach classes. No classes and no grant funding equals an unpaid sabbatical. So there's got to be a way to fund this if we're going to set it up as a small test project that may tell us if researching these alternative therapies is something we want to pursue more broadly going forward.

"You need someone to pay you for the semester?"

Mandy shrugged. "To put it bluntly, yes."

Dane shifted in his chair. There had to be a way to make this happen. There had to be a game plan. He excelled at game plans. That's what Provident College paid *him* for.

But never had any game been on the line in the same way Cole's future was on the line. One game, one season...none of that compared to needing to win the game that was *the rest of Cole's life.*

"I know of some Grad Assistant positions open in the athletic department. Want to be a GA for a semester? I could ask around."

"I don't really think I'd be an asset to the football team trying to come up with a two-minute drill." She gestured idly with her hands as she spoke. "But do you think there might be someone over there interested in alternative therapies for concussion rehabilitation? Again, this isn't an exact match with my specialty, but there's enough overlap because brain health is important across the board."

Now that, Dane could agree with. A lifetime of sports had taught him that injuries were part of life in athletics. But too often, coaches and trainers kept doing things the same way, year in and year out. In a lot of cases, there were new and better ideas—but they hadn't been distilled down to an easily-understood protocol.

"Let me ask around," he said.

Mandy's broad smile pushed aside the uneasiness which had flashed in his heart and mind just a few minutes ago.

"Great," she said. "I'll make my calls to the neurology department at Provident Medical. Then we can circle back and get moving. Hang tight, Cole. There will be some light at the end of the tunnel soon."

Dane wanted to believe in Mandy's parting message of hope. But what if he couldn't find a way to get her therapy project funded somehow?

They were talking about his son. About his son's future. Dane couldn't let that light at the end of the tunnel be a train. He had to find a way.

MANDY SQUINTED AGAINST the sunlight as she drove across the island from Provident College, silently cursing the fact that she'd left her sunglasses behind on her desk.

Mandy's mind kept turning over and over—but she couldn't hang on to the thoughts long enough to chain them together and make a plan. Without conscious prompting, her left hand slid off the steering wheel and flicked up on the turn signal. She rolled up to the stop sign, then fluidly moved the steering wheel toward the left, turning the corner.

Cats.

She needed cats.

Cats would solve this conundrum.

Specifically, spending an hour or two playing with the orphaned cats at the Port Provident Animal Shelter would give Mandy some mindless time to knit together the different threads crisscrossing her mind.

The bell on the door jingled as Mandy stepped inside. A head quickly popped up above the desk in the reception area.

"Hey there, Mandy!" Becca Reeder, the director of the Port Provident Animal Shelter stood up from the floor and showed off a grimy tennis ball that barely bore any resemblance to the chartreuse sphere it had once been. "Cookie's ball rolled under the desk. He made it pretty clear that either he was retrieving it, or I was. And you know Cookie. The chances were high that his method of retrieval would have included trying to flip the desk over with his nose. Anything for that tennis ball."

The Labrador retriever next to Becca nodded his fluffy head and licked the toy with a grateful slurp, then chomped down on two-thirds of the alien-shaped entertainment and trotted away.

Mandy and Becca laughed at the same time.

"I love Cookie's unending devotion to his tennis ball," Mandy said with a smile, watching Cookie's contented tail wag back and forth as he disappeared around the corner.

Becca raised her eyebrows in an understanding salute. "Having a tennis ball got Cookie through military service in Iraq and through Hurricane Hope. It kind of makes me wish we could give everyone a tennis ball. Think of how much happier and more well-adjusted we would all be."

"Oh, definitely. I wish a tennis ball could solve the problems in front of me right now." Mandy signed in on the volunteer roster.

Becca raised her eyebrows high and let her mouth twitch off toward the left side of her face. The quizzical expression made Mandy laugh.

"Problems? As in plural?"

"Completely plural. The program I was supposed to be researching with this summer got shut down due to funding concerns at the government level over in Europe."

"Okay, that's one." Becca smoothed her Port Provident Animal Shelter T-shirt over the tiniest of baby bumps. "What else?"

"I've been asked to help put together a brain rehab program for a PC student who is suffering from post-concussive syndrome. I want to help, but there's no budget for anything—including my own paycheck, since I was supposed to be funded by the research program this summer. So...I have no research, no income, and no resources with which to help this student. It all feels a little overwhelming right now. Which is why I came here—to play with kittens. That seems like a very adult thing to do, right?"

Becca made a note next to Mandy's signature in the log. "Kittens are always the right answer. We got a new gray one in today. She was found up in a tree on Avenue R. You're probably going to want to take her home with you."

"Becca, hush. Don't tempt me, please. If I don't figure out the paycheck situation, I might be eating cat food this summer. I can't afford another tiny mouth to feed."

"Fair. All I do is eat these days, so I completely understand. I'm pretty sure Ross thinks I eat more than his entire unit in Iraq. I put away a large chicken fried steak last weekend—and still had room for dessert. One thing is for sure, this baby is not going to be lacking for nutrients to use to grow."

Hearing the joy in her friend's voice made Mandy smile. It felt good to let the worry wash away and to focus on the good in the world.

"Have you thought about getting some kind of corporate sponsor? Ross has done that with his military dog re-homing program. It's been very helpful."

Hope flickered in Mandy's heart for an instant. She could feel it deep inside, like a kitten's purr. "That might be a real idea. Who do you think would want to sponsor neuroeducation research?"

"Hmm...I don't know. My specialty is dogs and cats. But if anyone in this town knows who has grant money, it's the Peoples Family Foundation. They know every charitable dollar in this town. Don't you work with Jake Peoples' wife?"

The hopeful purring in Mandy's soul began to rise. "Oh my gosh, Gracie—yes. You're right. I do. I need to talk to Gracie. She can help point me in the right direction."

"But first," Becca said with a smile, "you need to go in the direction of the kittens. Third door on the left."

"You're right, you know." Mandy opened the half-door to walk behind the counter and head back toward the shelter's cat zone.

"About what?"

"Kittens are always the right answer. I have some calls in over at Provident Medical Center to see if I can pull some strings for testing. But that still wouldn't solve the problem of allowing me to assist Cole as fully as I'd like. And ff I hadn't come here today, I would never have thought to talk to Gracie—which just might be the connection I need to take care of everything. So, once again, kittens save the day."

Becca raised her stainless steel water bottle. "To kittens."

"To kittens. And the opportunity to still do research this summer that can make a difference."

Chapter Three

"HEY THERE! YOUR ASSISTANT told me I'd find you out here," Mandy said.

She leaned over the dugout rail at Tidal Waves Ballpark, known to everyone on the Provident College campus as "The Splash."

Dane turned around and looked up. He adjusted his sunglasses as a warm smile crossed his face at the sight of her. "She was right. If you're lookin' for me, and you can't find me, the chances are I'm down here on the field."

Mandy shielded her eyes from the sun with the palm of her hand. "So, how's the season going?"

"Good." The brim of Dane's baseball cap bounced slightly, moving up and down. "If we can just keep doing what we're doing, we should be invited to a post-season regional."

"Wow, that's great. I have a lot of good memories from watching my brother play as a kid. It seems like so long ago."

Dane's own eyes took on a bit of a faraway stare. "Yeah, the years go by fast."

Mandy looked out at the green semi-circle of grass reaching back to the outfield wall. "They certainly do. But then, sometimes, it's good to stop and take stock of the moment. And today is one of those times."

"It is?" Dane leaned on the rail.

"Yes. This is a great moment. I spoke with Dr. Brennan, the head of the neurology department at Provident Medical Center. He pulled some strings with Dr. Martie Post, a neuropsychologist who specializes in TBIs and post-concussive syndrome. Dr. Post had a cancellation on her schedule and she's going to be able to evaluate Cole in her office this week."

"This week? Really?"

Mandy wanted to squeal a little bit, but she felt like she needed to rein it in. She still had to be professional. This was all tied to her research. She couldn't be acting like a teenager at a rock concert—even if formal neuropsych evaluations excited her far more these days than a teen idol on stage in a pair of tight jeans ever could.

"Really. It's just amazing. A total blessing. A God thing. These appointments usually take months to get."

At the mention of the word "God," Mandy saw Dane's chin tilt downward. She couldn't see the track of his eyes behind the sunglasses, but there was no mistaking the scuff of the toe of his cleat in the dirt.

"So what's this God thing entail?"

Mandy didn't want to say Dane's voice was sarcastic, but the tone had definitely gone flat. She stopped herself from saying anything further. She wasn't here to research Dane or his thoughts on miracles in everyday life. She was here for two very specific reasons—to get Cole's grades out of the danger zone and hopefully get him back on the team, and to hopefully parlay that into more extensive research for her own future and career.

"It's an all-day appointment. They'll interview him and do a battery of tests to pinpoint his strengths and weaknesses with regard to his brain functions. After the results are assessed, we'll know more about what he can and can't do and where we should focus his rehabilitation."

The cloud that had settled over Dane's demeanor dissipated. "Wow, Dr. McGovern. That sounds incredible. I don't even know what to say. Thank you for making all that happen so quickly."

"Well, it wasn't really me," she replied before remembering her resolution to not allude to *the God thing* anymore in front of Dane.

"It feels good to be moving forward, finally. I honestly don't know what to say."

Mandy reached back and grabbed her ponytail, then tightened it. "Well, you can start by just calling me Mandy. Dr. McGovern sounds way too formal for a conversation on a baseball field."

The coach nodded. "Sure, but only if you'll call me Dane."

Mandy took in a deep breath of fresh ballpark air, happy for the moment. Just knowing that even with all the disappointment she'd seen in her own week, she now had the opportunity to bring happiness and hope to someone else's week—well, it seemed to take the edge off her own wounds.

There was still some good in the world, after all.

A line of ball players ran past Dane in the dugout, giving him high-fives as they ducked into the door leading to the locker room under the stadium. "Good job today, guys. See you tomorrow morning in the weight room."

Dane shouted encouragement at his players, then turned back to Mandy. He paused for a moment. Again, the reflective lenses of the sunglasses hid the tracks of his gaze from her, but something in her stomach stirred. The flip and flap of little butterflies told Mandy that the coach was studying her.

"Practice is over—and I don't know about you, but I've been thinking about pizza for the last hour. Would you like to join me, and then maybe you can tell me more about these appointments? I feel like as a coach I should have heard of some of this concussion treatment stuff, but I haven't. And as a dad...well..."

Dane's voice trailed off. Mandy could hear some indistinguishable shouting from the players below, but otherwise, the ballpark was still for a moment. He seemed so serious. Evaluating personality traits was part of her work, and right now, she wanted to take out a tablet and start making notes on Dane Vasquez.

He was definitely a concerned dad and a good coach. But the way he'd go from chatty and engaged to quiet and thoughtful on a dime...well, it set Mandy's researcher radar off.

There was something there. She knew it, just like Scooby Doo could sniff out trouble the minute he hopped from the door of the Mystery Machine.

Scooby always seemed to solve the puzzle with the help of some Scooby Snacks. Maybe pizza would be the missing link for her pondering.

"Sure," Mandy said. "Pizza sounds great. I mean, I'll never turn down pizza. Besides, it's not like I'm teaching classes this semester and need to finish getting things ready. What did you have in mind?"

"Meet me at The Seahorse in like twenty minutes or so?"

Mandy could feel her mouth begin to water at the thought of future carbs. "Mmm. I love The Seahorse. But can you give me half an hour? I've got to get back across campus to get my car out of the faculty parking lot."

"Sounds like a plan. See you there."

THE SEAHORSE WAS A legendary Port Provident institution that had been cooking up the best of guilty pleasure food with a view of the Gulf of Mexico for more than two decades. Serving both locals and beach-going tourists alike, The Seahorse made sure no one's craving for pizza, burgers, or fries went unsatisfied in while on Provident Island.

Dane remembered stopping here every summer when he came to visit his cousin Rigo. They'd hang out in a booth at the back, drinking pitchers of soda and talking about only two things: girls and baseball. Walking through the door of The Seahorse always took Dane back to a time when he didn't have any worries—and he didn't have any concern for anyone other than himself.

That self-centered adolescence migrated into his twenties—and sadly, even beyond—and shaped more of his life than he'd cared to admit.

But he'd made up his mind to do things differently, to change the trajectory of the decades behind him, and maybe—just maybe—be the man his son needed in his life.

The bell on the front door jingled, and as Dane looked up, Mandy walked in. He couldn't get enough of that ponytail. Something about it made him smile. Every. Single. Time.

When it came to noticing women, Dane definitely had a type, and never before had he considered himself a "ponytail man." His life in Port Provident had definitely changed him—in ways he never dreamed possible.

"Mmm. This place is just like a warm hug. Calzones are kind of my love language." Mandy slid across the red vinyl bench opposite Dane.

A light blinked in his head. *Calzones good. Noted.*

"I'm probably going to have to get to the weight room before the guys in the morning, but I'm pretty sure it will be worth it," Dane reciprocated Mandy's appreciation for the local joint. "Do you come here often?"

She shook her head with a laugh. "Not as much as I'd like to, trust me. But my job doesn't give me the opportunity to workout or run sprints to atone for my bad behavior."

Her words reminded Dane of his earlier thoughts. Atonement. That was exactly the word he'd been looking for earlier. He was on this quest for Cole because he needed to be a dad. He needed to do something right for once. He needed to atone for all the times he hadn't been there.

"It's not as glamorous as you'd think." Dane pushed the menu off to the corner of the table. He didn't even need to look at it to know what he'd be ordering. "But tell me more about your job. What is it exactly that you do?"

"I specialize in inclusive classroom settings and teaching future educators how to create those," she said simply.

"I'm a sports guy. What does that mean in English?"

"It means that every child deserves an environment in which they can learn. My goal is to teach our education students how to create those areas where children are comfortable getting the accommodations they need and the teachers are empowered and equipped to provide that experience and a great education to go along with it. I teach things like classroom management strategies, how to talk to children about disabilities, how to come up with physical arrangements in the classroom that lead to success. And I hope to instill in them a curiosity and a desire for research to stay on the cutting edge because we have a lot of kids in school today with conditions like ADHD, autism, and more—and there are always new ideas and approaches we're learning for how to support these students to do their best work and be successful."

It sounded pretty important to him, and in a way, he felt he could relate. "I think as a coach, I have similar goals. Different guys are motivated in different ways. My job is to reach them and get them to where they need to be so they can meet the needs we have as a team, while still meeting their personal goals. There's a lot of balancing."

Mandy tapped the table lightly. "Exactly. This is just taking that basic tenet of education—helping students learn and thrive—and then going a step further with it. Some barriers to classroom success can be in the brain, and others can be physical. But it's up to educators today to work with things like 504s and IEPs—and even to help out and recognize areas that can be helped, even if there's not a formal arrangement governing the student's education."

"So how does your research tie into that?" Dane could tell Mandy was passionate about her work. As she explained her role in the education department, the timbre of her voice became deeper and more rich. Listening to her was almost like biting into the sweetest strawberry at the height of summer. There was just something superlative about *how* she explained it, not just the words she spoke.

"Well, I've always been interested in low-intervention therapies. Using things like essential oil diffusers in the classroom, or changing seating arrangements from chairs to balls. How can we use music and scheduled periods of active movement to benefit kids and their natural energy? Two years ago, I was doing research on diffusing essential oils in the classroom and I became hooked on the science behind the oils. Monoterpenes, sesquiterpenes, utilizing the limbic system to stimulate the different areas of the brain...there's a lot there."

Dane waved his hands. "Whoa, whoa. Monosesquiterrapins? Isn't the terrapin the mascot at the University of Maryland? Isn't that a fancy way of saying turtle? Are you putting turtles in the classroom?"

A throaty, high-pitched laugh burst out of Mandy. "Not terrapins. Terpenes. Terpenes are organic hydrocarbons found in plants. You'll often find them used in fragrances or flavorings. But they can influence neurotransmitters, affect mood, things like that."

"You're still kind of speaking a foreign language. You've got a jock here at the table, remember?"

"Hold on. I've got something that will help." Mandy grabbed her purse and began to rummage inside.

"You carry these not-really-a-terrapin things in your purse? Is that legal?" Dane eyed the professor skeptically.

"Terpenes. And yes, it's totally legal." She held up a brown glass bottle with an orange label, then removed the white plastic lid and held it out to him. "Smell this."

Dane did as he was told.

"Orangey. A little bit lemony too."

She nodded. "Right. And how does that make you feel?"

"Pretty happy, I guess. I like the smell of lemons. They remind me of my aunt's clean kitchen and drinking lemonade at the ballpark as a kid."

"Aaah." She waved the small bottle under her own nose and breathed in deeply. "Exactly. Terpenes at work. Citrus oils contain a terpene known as limonene. Limonene generally promotes good feelings, a rise in mood. When you smell blend of citrus oils like this, those limonene molecules travel up your nose and are processed by your limbic system, which is made up of several areas in your brain. Then your body triggers an appropriate response. So just by smelling this tiny bottle of oil, you triggered a memory in your brain of happiness and your hypothalamus was given the signal to relax and enjoy the moment. And all that happened without you ever taking a pill or being hooked up to a machine."

The corner of Dane's mouth twitched. "That's kind of amazing."

"Isn't it? And if we can help students stimulate the areas of their brain that keep them relaxed or alert or more at-ease and happy, then we can impact their productivity in the classroom and their general well-being. It fascinates me."

She fascinated him.

It hit Dane like connecting a bat with the perfect fastball streaking across the center of the plate. The observation happened so fast, he didn't have time to let anything but instinct take over. There was no time to think about it or analyze it.

He just let the realization hit the right spot and fly.

But in baseball, he knew what to do. That perfectly-hit ball would fly over the bases, cut above the outfield and soar past the wall. It would advance runners, score points, and win the game.

He always knew what to do in baseball. But in life? That was another story.

Dane Vasquez struck out every single time.

"Did I lose you again?" Mandy looked across the table, one eyebrow raised at a slight angle.

Dane tried to shake off the convoluted train of thought in his head. "No, not really."

"Not really?"

"No. Oily terrapins can make you happy. I got that part."

"Or focused, or more relaxed, or other things," she said softly.

"Can it fix stuff?" Dane wondered out loud before he even realized he'd verbalized the thought in his heart.

"Well, I think it can. The brain is an amazing thing. I know you're worried about Cole, but he's in good hands. We just have to trust the process and have faith for his healing. Like I said back at the ballpark, there's a God thing at work here. I don't believe in coincidences."

At that, Dane lifted his head and looked up at her. "I don't either. But I don't know if I believe the God thing, either."

"Why not?" Mandy asked softly.

He might as well be honest. She was putting her time and effort into Cole's recovery. Mandy at least deserved straightforward answers so she knew the full extent of the mess she was aligning herself with.

"This was supposed to be my chance."

"Like in baseball? This season? Are you hoping to win a championship?"

Dane shrugged. "You're not a true competitor if you don't start every season hoping to win a championship. But no, I meant with Cole. Having him here was supposed to be my chance to build a relationship with him. To finally man up and do the dad thing. To coach my kid in ball like I never took the time to do before."

He paused, but decided to finish coming clean before she could interject and keep him from getting it off his chest.

"I haven't been there for him. I let his mom and stepdad raise him. His stepdad coached T-ball. I was always out chasing a dream, or women, or whatever was in front of me that day. Two and a half years ago, I got a Christmas card from their family. It was picture-perfect—his mom, stepdad, twin half-sisters, and there was my son standing right behind them. In their Christmas letter, it mentioned that Cole had been attracting attention from Major League Baseball scouts and he was trying to decide if he wanted to play college ball or go straight to the minors. I broke down in tears. I didn't even know. I'd missed it all. By then, I'd retired from the league and was coaching at a junior college in California. I called my cousin Rigo, telling him what a mess I'd made of my whole life and I needed a change. He told me about this job. The coach had left Provident College after the hurricane—they'd cancelled the season and everything was a mess here too. It seemed fitting. I needed to start over and so did this team. After I got the job, the first recruiting trip I made was back to Chicago to recruit Cole. I wanted the chance to coach my kid, and he actually said yes. But now it's all ruined. He's here, but he's injured and not playing and I don't even know how to be a dad or to fix this."

Mandy reached across the table and laid her hands on top of Dane's. He felt the curve of her fingertips graze the side of his knuckle and come to rest on the edge of his palm. Her touch was as light as the weight in his heart was heavy.

Dane stilled for a moment, thinking about the opposites at play and counting each slow breath.

"That's a God thing too."

He looked at her hands and his hands and then turned his gaze upward.

"What is?" he said.

"Restoring the broken. Rebuilding relationships. That's maybe the biggest God thing of them all."

Chapter Four

"WHY DOES TECHNOLOGY always do this to me?" Mandy stood in front of her printer, willing it to function just by the sheer amount of frustration in her voice. It wasn't working. "Ugh. You hate me don't you?"

"Well no, not really. I enjoy working with you. Is there something I should know?" Gracie Garcia-Peoples laughed as she walked into Mandy's office. After completing her Master's in bilingual education last year at Provident College, Gracie had joined the education department staff as a part-time lecturer. She and Mandy had become fast friends both through their work in the department and the Faculty-Staff Bible study group that met on campus weekly.

"I just need to get this consent form printed off, but no, the printer of obnoxiousness is at it again, trying to foil every plan I have. I think that every Monday morning, the first thing I'm going to do when I walk in the building is to leave a requisition request for a new printer on Roger's desk. Eventually, budget or no budget, he'll cave."

"Ah, the old wear them down by being annoying trick?" Gracie turned around and waved behind her. "Email it to me, and I will print it for you. *Vamonos.*"

Mandy ran to her computer and sent the quick email, then followed Gracie down the hall as she'd requested.

"Thank you for saving me from technology," Mandy said to her friend gratefully. "If I don't get rolling, I won't make it to Provident Medical on time, and I have to get this signed before the appointment starts."

Gracie took the last sheet of paper off the printer and handed the small stack to Mandy. "What on earth are you talking about? I heard you were staying here but that you weren't on the schedule for anything this semester. What do you need consent forms for?"

"Good news travels fast, huh?"

"I know losing your funding and research trip like that had to be very disappointing. But at least you get some kind of a break. You were pretty burned out last semester, with all of your responsibilities. Between teaching and advising your group of thesis students and chairing the Student Judicial Affairs Committee, I honestly don't know how you kept your head above water. For some reason, last semester seem to just be supersized for you. I don't know why you had so many judicial affairs cases, or why none of your thesis students could get a break, but nothing seemed to be simple for you the last few months."

"I think this may wind up being my most complex term of all," Mandy said, lowering her voice just slightly.

Gracie leaned back, bracing herself on the edge of her desk. "No classes, no research, no grading, no teaching. You and I must have different definitions of the word complex, *amiga*."

Mandy took half a step backwards into the hallway. She looked right, she looked left. Stepping back into Gracie's office, Mandy quietly closed the door behind her.

"Okay... Now I'm worried. Is something going on? Do you need some help? You're the most open person I know. You don't keep secrets behind closed doors," Gracie said.

Mandy hesitated. She'd been thinking about this – about Dane's confession regarding his relationship with his son – since the minute he served it up in the restaurant. "Do you know the baseball coach?"

"Dane Vasquez?"

Mandy nodded.

"Sure I know him. His cousin Rigo is married to my sister Gloria."

"Are you serious?" Mandy couldn't keep the sound of surprise out of her voice.

"Yeah." Gracie waved her hand dismissively. "It's a Hispanic thing. And a small-town thing. We're all like a second cousin, twice-removed or somebody's aunt's cousin's brother. It's part of having big families and a tight-knit community."

"Okay, then never mind." She lifted the group of papers. "Thanks for printing this for me."

Gracie made it to the door in two swift steps. "Not so fast there, *amiga*." She leaned forward and pressed her hand on the door, trapping Mandy inside the office.

"Gracie, I'm gonna be late."

"Tough. Spill it. What are you talking about?"

"He just said something at dinner last night that made me think, that's all." Maybe if she kept it short and sweet, Gracie would let her out of the office. *Don't give her anything, McGovern, and she will get tired of asking—just like Roger and those printer requests.*

"Wait. Wait. Wait." Gracie's eyes popped open like a super-sized pancake.

Instantly, Mandy knew she'd taken the wrong approach. *New plan. Stay silent. Don't give her any ammo.*

"Dinner last night? You had dinner with Dane?"

"Mmm-hmm." She could make sounds. That would be okay. That wouldn't violate the "don't say too much" plan. In reality, it was practically like saying nothing at all.

"You can't just leave it at that."

Mandy had seen the stare on Gracie's face before...on Gracie's mother, the Garcia family matriarch who owned Huarache's, one of Port Provident's most popular casual Mexican food restaurants. That look was genetic. And it was not going to be denied.

"I'm helping him with a project." That was honest.

"Over dinner? At the faculty dining room?" A while back, Mandy and Gracie were discussing their siblings. Gracie mentioned that her older sister, Gloria, had missed her calling as an FBI interrogator. Perhaps Gloria wasn't the only one in the family who had that calling.

Mandy pursed her lips. "No."

"Oh, come on, Mandy!" Gracie rolled her eyes as she choked down a laugh. "You can't keep a secret, and you know it. You talk about this all the time—about how your students rat you out for being a big softie. Have you ever been able to not give an extension on a project, no matter how ridiculous the excuse?"

Resistance was futile. Gracie spoke the truth.

"Fine. We ate at The Seahorse."

Gracie nodded. "Okay, now we're getting somewhere. There's a big difference between a fancy seafood dinner at Porter's and a twelve-inch pepperoni pizza at The Seahorse. So what's the project?"

Cornered, Mandy conceded defeat. "His son Cole. Do you know what's going on with him?"

"At Sunday dinner last week, Rigo mentioned that Cole's grades last semester were bad and they haven't cleared him to play again."

"Right. He's about to lose his scholarship."

"But where do you come in? You're not a tutor."

Mandy shook her head. "He doesn't need a tutor. We're getting him a neuropsychological evaluation at Provident Medical today, and I am pretty sure the results are going to show memory deficits and executive function issues. And I just so happen to work with classroom accommodations and brain-based challenges in students."

Gracie's jaw dropped slightly. "Wow. I've talked about it in passing with Rigo a few times, but I never connected two and two together. I should have introduced you to him a long time ago."

"Well, I was supposed to be on a plane for Europe today, so I wouldn't have been able to help."

Her colleague took in a deep breath. "Mandy, maybe that's it. It's a God thing. Maybe the door for the research closed, but this one opened."

Mandy couldn't deny the sensation in her gut as Gracie spoke the exact same words Mandy herself had said to Dane yesterday. It felt as though fireworks were going off, the spark of something greater than anything she could accomplish on her own.

A God thing.

"You think so?" Mandy fished for the definitive confirmation.

"He needs help, Mandy. He's been told he'll get better with time, and it's not happening. Maybe with your insight and knowledge, you can get him on the path he needs to be on in order to turn this thing around." Gracie shifted her weight from foot to foot. "But what about it is bothering you? Something was. Is it Dane?"

Mandy took a steadying breath. So much for the resolution not to say much. She'd wanted to keep her mouth shut, but her friend had just poked a hole in every single defense she had.

"Well, it's crazy, but I used the exact words last night that you used—maybe it's a God thing. He'd said that he had a rocky relationship with his son and he didn't even know how to be a parent or to fix what was going on. I said that when we're at the end of what we know to do, that's when God can step in and restore. He just shut down after that. Changed the subject. Started talking about pizza and all the weird hole-in-the-wall places he ate while he was traveling on the road, playing with minor league baseball teams."

Gracie leaned against the door. "He's a good person, and he's trying to make a fresh start here in Port Provident. I think he wants to leave his past baggage behind. But he's the type who relies on one thing and one thing only—himself. There are no God things in his life. Only Dane things."

Mandy let Gracie's assessment settle for a moment. It made perfect sense.

"That helps." She waved the consent document between the two of them. "But if I don't get moving, he and Cole won't be able to rely on me, either."

"Understood." Gracie stepped back from the door and put her hand on the knob, turning it slightly and cracking the door open. "If you need anything—advice, a listening ear, or just a supportive prayer—don't hesitate to ask. Cole's a good kid. I really hope you can help him."

"I do too, Gracie. I'm going to give it my best shot." Mandy stepped out into the hallway, then paused. "And then I'll let God do the rest."

"DON'T BE NERVOUS, SON. You've taken lots of tests before. This is just another one. Nothing more, nothing less." Dane squeezed Cole's hand lightly. His son had been quiet all morning.

"I guess I want to know what's going on—but if it's bad news, like if it's permanent or something, I don't really want to know, you know?"

"I get it. I really do." Dane understood Cole's hesitation. He felt it himself. What if today was the last day they could say "with time, it'll all get back to normal"? What if today was the day they found out things in Cole's life would never be normal again?

What if today was the day they lost hope?

The heavy door to the quiet office opened with a click. Dane looked up from the oatmeal-colored wall he'd been staring down in a daze.

Mandy waved as she slipped inside. "I'm glad I caught you before you went in."

Dane didn't understand her whole "God thing" commentary from last night—how on earth could a brain injury be any kind of God thing?—but he couldn't deny there was something calming about her presence. He just felt better when he was around her. Something about Mandy McGovern's light spirit made him feel like things would be okay.

He knew that was most likely a misguided interpretation of some wishful thinking based on her area of teaching, but for now, it was a shred of hope. He was going to take what he could find.

She laid some papers on the table in front of Dane and Cole. "This is the consent form for how we'll be working together. It will explain what we're going to be doing, how we're going to work together, how your privacy is governed, and what I'll do with the information that's collected. It's not a very long document, but I need you to read and sign before we can officially work together."

Cole picked up the document and began to scan it. "Do you have a pen?"

"I've got one in my purse somewhere. Read the forms carefully while I dig for it. I want you to feel like you understand and support how we're going to work together." She turned to Dane. "And while he's got to be the one to sign it, since he's eighteen, I'd like for you to read it too, so you understand everything as well."

Mandy opened her purse wide and began to move the contents around. Dane picked up the papers as Cole read each one, then laid it back down on the table.

"Okay," Dane said simply.

"You don't have any questions?" Mandy asked, handing Cole the black ballpoint pen.

"No. I trust your recommendations. I don't think you'd do anything that would hurt Cole's chances of recovery."

Mandy collected the pages that Cole had signed and initialed. "Not at all. These are low-intervention methods. They may help, they may not. But I don't foresee a situation where they'd cause further problems."

"Then let's do it," Cole said, his words underscored with conviction.

"Great. I believe in you, Cole." Mandy handed one more paper to him. "This is the last form. It allows me to get access to your schedule and visit your professors on your behalf to help set up any accommodations you might need this coming semester."

Cole scrawled his name at the bottom of the page with a flourish. "Cool. Thanks for helping me."

Dane was blown away by how Cole was taking everything in stride today. In his late teens, Dane was running away from his problems without so much as a glance backward—a trait which led to the eventual estrangement between father and son. He wished he'd been one half the man back then that his son was today.

The door at the back of the waiting room opened. "Cole Vasquez? We're ready. Come on back and let's get started."

A woman in a navy sweater twin-set and dress slacks beckoned at the patient.

"Good luck, Cole. Knock it out of the park." Dane stood and leaned over to embrace his son. He could feel a lump forming in his throat. It felt rough and jagged—much like all of his emotions about this situation lately. Nothing had been easy or straightforward on this journey.

"I brought Cole to Port Provident with the intent of building a relationship with my son. All along, I thought the obstacle between us was me—was my ego, my pride, my desire to be a ball player," Dane said as the door closed behind Cole. "Once I realized that and got it out of my way, I thought everything would be smooth. I never planned on anything like this. I never planned on loving this kid so much that it scared me. But I'm scared now. I'm scared for him. I'm scared for us. What if we never get to build the relationship I brought him here for?"

He closed his eyes.

Lightly, a hand slipped on his shoulder. The palm curved around the arch at the top of the arm. Long, narrow fingers came to rest down his bicep. The hand didn't pat, it didn't squeeze. It didn't do anything besides just *be*.

For his whole life, stillness had infuriated Dane. He'd always been on the move, since long before he could even speak. His need for activity had led him to baseball very early in life.

But right now, the stillness seemed right.

Mandy hadn't said a word, but somehow, she'd let Dane know she was there and he wasn't struggling with his thoughts and his second guesses alone.

"It might not be the exact relationship you thought brought him here for. But maybe it'll be the one you need."

Dane opened his eyes and turned slightly to face Mandy. Her hand brushed down the length of his arm until it dropped back by her side.

Maybe he needed more than the chance to get to know his son. Maybe he needed the chance to get to know this woman, too.

CRUNCH.

Crunch.

Crunch.

Mandy took note of each foot-fall on the trail surrounding the Provident College campus. She tried to run at least two miles, three days a week after work. It cleared her head to listen to nothing but the sound of her feet moving forward.

She desperately needed to get her arms around this idea of moving forward. Lately, she'd had her fill of unexpected shocks and disappointments. In the midst of that mess, though, she'd been given the opportunity to help Cole Vasquez navigate his own challenges.

She might not be able to do work that would lead to helping people around the world like she'd thought, but if she could change one person's world, maybe that would be enough.

The gravel on the trail crunched beneath her hot pink running shoes and the early summer sun warmed her arms.

They pumped back and forth in time with the movement of her feet. For a moment, she was lost in the routine.

"Mandy!" A familiar voice called out.

She turned her head and saw Dane sprinting across the grass toward her. She slowed down and gave him a moment to catch up.

"Hey. Have you heard anything from Cole's test?"

"I'm about to head there now to pick him up. He said he was tired, but overall, he was doing as well as could be expected. Do you want to come with me?"

The smile on Dane's face was almost a complete one-eighty from the expression he'd carried this morning. It caused her own mouth to curve gently upward. Maybe they were all turning a corner this afternoon.

"Ugh. I'm all stinky." She gestured at the sweat stain on her tank top. "I don't think this is the aromatherapy we had in mind to try on Cole."

Dane's warm grin didn't change. "You're beautiful."

Mandy took a step back, unsure quite how to take his compliment. "You've spent too much time on the field today, Coach Vasquez. The summer heat has fried your brain."

"Nope." He shook his head. "And I think I asked you to call me Dane."

Something in his voice caught her attention and Mandy looked him over. He might have been crazy to think her sweaty workout clothes were high fashion, but there was no doubt at all that he made shorts and tight-fitting athletic wear look ready for a runway.

"Hey...can I ask you something?" Dane caught up to Mandy's moderate jog in a matter of a few steps.

"Sure. Is it about Cole's testing today? I know all of that is a lot to take in and keep straight."

"No. Not about the testing—but about something else you said. It's been on my mind."

Mandy's mind hit the rewind button, trying to come up with some idea of what they could have talked about that would have lingered on his mind, yet had nothing to do with Cole and the testing.

"Well, sure...shoot. What's up?"

"You said the other day that you thought this was all a God thing—everything happens for a reason, or something like that. You know, whatever church people say." He paused, and Mandy could hear him starting and stopping phrases under his breath, trying to come up with the right words.

She looked away from the trail with a cock of her head. "What church people say?"

"Yeah...I mean...I don't know. I've never been a church person. But don't they say things like that? That there's always a plan or some reason?"

She heard a searching in his words.

"Well, I guess you could put it like that. There's a verse that says 'All things work to good for those who love the Lord and are called according to His purposes.'"

Dane snapped his fingers. "Exactly. Something like that."

"So what's your question?"

"I think...I think this happened for a reason." The pace of his words was measured. "I think...Mandy, do you think what's happened to Cole is punishment for me? Do you think God's punishing me for living the life I have? I never cared. I was never there for the people who needed me. I was all ego, all about me. And now, I've tried to turn things around so I can get to know my son and it just feels like there's one roadblock after another. I can't help but think that I'm being punished for my past—I can't have the relationship I want with my son because I've waited until it's all too late. Do you think that's what this is?"

Dane's search for answers pierced Mandy's heart like an icicle. Sharp and cold, his raw questions and the tone in which he'd asked them left no doubt that these thoughts were the true sentiments in his soul.

He believed what he was saying and was just looking to her for confirmation.

Mandy didn't know what to say, except to give him some of the "churchy" phrases that he clearly didn't think much of. One by one, verses she'd memorized in Sunday School or Vacation Bible School came to mind.

But she knew he wasn't going to accept a laundry list of scripture as an answer. She couldn't answer this wrong. She couldn't push him away or further confirm his hunch that "churchy" people just spoke in old-sounding phrases.

She put one foot in front of the other for a few more paces, then chewed ever so slightly on her bottom lip as she decided what she needed to say. Mandy took a deep breath and asked God to help her not sound "churchy," but instead to be the friend who spoke the truth and the reassurance that Dane needed to hear.

"No, I don't think that's it at all. Here's what we do know—the Bible calls God our Father. Think about your relationship with Cole. Think about the lengths you've gone to in order to repair your relationship with him. You've turned your life around, left bad habits, gotten a new job, moved across the country, and convinced him to join you for an opportunity that would give you both the chance to know each other and to play the game you both love."

Dane nodded his head, but didn't interject.

Mandy slowed the pace of her steps and turned her head slightly. She wanted to see Dane's reaction to her words.

The muscle at the back of his jaw clenched. Then it locked. Then it tightened. Mandy could see the muscle fibers separate and line up like soldiers along the line of bone. So much tension pulsed along that meridian that Mandy wondered if his response would actually be an explosion.

"Yeah," he said simply as he stared at the curve ahead in the trail. "But don't you think I'm right?"

She shook her head and stopped jogging completely. When Dane realized Mandy was no longer at his side, he stopped too and then went backwards a few steps to join her.

"Absolutely not," she said. "I don't agree with you at all. The Bible tells us that God is our Father. And if you would turn your whole life upside down for the chance to get to know your son and to coach him in just one baseball game...how much farther will the God who created the universe and everything in it go to develop a relationship with you? He's not going to do all that just so he can yell at you and make you feel badly about yourself."

She prayed he could hear nothing but the conviction and care in her heart, not condemnation.

Dane tilted his head and looked at the blue sky stretched above the Provident College campus. His hands were clenched in balled fists alongside his weight-toned and tanned legs.

"I've screwed up one thing after another for my whole life, Mandy. I just don't think you understand."

"Maybe I don't understand everything you've done, Dane. But I am certain that the God that I know—the God that I talk about—has seen every single one of your screw-ups. And he still pursued you here, to Provident College, and to a table at lunch in the faculty dining room so you could eventually hear these words and drop this weight from your shoulders. There's nothing that Cole could do to make you love him less, simply because you're his father and you want to know him. And in that same way, there's nothing you could do to make God love you less because He's your Father and he wants to know you."

Mandy reached out her hand. For a moment, it seemed like a very solitary gesture. Dane didn't move. But inside, Mandy knew she couldn't pull away.

She'd extended this gesture of support. She would not take it back. Instead, she decided to just wait there on the gravel-and-dirt trail until Dane accepted the help he didn't even know he'd asked for.

Dane looked down at his feet, then pulled his gaze up to where he connected with Mandy. His eyes, the color of dark sand, sent a flash of lightning from her head to her toes.

She felt the connection. It was as real as if there were an actual wire between them, moving the energy back and forth.

He put his palm on top of hers and threaded his fingers between each of her own digits, deepening the link she felt. This was not just a simple helping hand. She was used to observation and study, but she didn't know how to fully classify everything she was feeling.

"Let's go get Cole," Dane said. "I want to talk to my son."

Chapter Five

DANE LET OFF THE BRAKE and began to inch down the circular drive in front of Cole's dormitory. He turned to Mandy, sitting in the passenger seat beside him.

"Man, I hate leaving him like this. I feel like I should make him chicken noodle soup or something. He just seems so wiped out."

Mandy kept her eyes glued to the door of the building as it closed behind Cole.

"I know how you feel. I want to give him a hug. Those tests use the whole brain—the parts that are injured, the parts that don't always get used. It's a full mental workout, and I'm told that at the end, it's like going through a marathon. Total rest is the best medicine. No lights, no sound, just time to repair and heal."

"I'd like to give him a hug too." Dane put on his blinker and turned on to the street. "I'm definitely going to check back in on him tonight."

"Will you let me know if he needs anything? I don't live too far from here."

"Of course. Thanks for the offer."

Mandy reached behind her head and adjusted her ponytail. "I'm going to go back to my office in a bit and pick up some things that I think might help him shake off the brain fog. Remember the terpenes?"

Dane's grin was as insolent as a pirate's. "Yeah, the science lesson."

She swatted at his arm. "There are a few things we could put in a diffuser in the room that would work as a passive therapy. Oils like cedarwood are calming and can facilitate rest, and cedarwood is also loaded in sesquiterpenes."

"Sooo...lots of turtles."

A short musical laugh came from Mandy's side of the car. "Lots and lots of turtles."

"I've got to head to the ballpark and start getting ready for tonight's game. I can drop you off at your office..." He thought of a better idea. He didn't want Mandy out of his sight yet. She'd completely changed everything about this day and had kept him calm on a day that had started full of agitation. "Or I can give you a tour of The Splash."

Dane smiled broadly, hopeful that he could convince her to spend a little more time with him.

"You know, I've never been to a game at The Splash."

He clutched a hand to his heart. "Mandy. That hurts. You've been at Provident College how long?"

She shrugged. "Teaching? Five years in the fall."

"Didn't you say you grew up watching baseball?"

"Yeah, my brother played all the way through college."

"But yet, you've never been to a game here?"

Her ponytail tossed, and as he caught the swish in the corner of his eye, it hypnotized him all over again. "Not a one. I think I've become too much of a homebody or a paper grader or something."

Dane stopped at a red light and looked straight at his passenger. "I thought you were an official crazy cat lady. It's time to get back to the ballpark, Mandy. Reconnect with something you love, something that's fun."

He loved looking at her face as the slow smile began to dawn on her lips. "You're right. I'd really like a tour of The Splash. Besides, if I get my things and head back to the dorm too soon, I'll probably wake Cole up."

Dane turned down the alley behind the athletic complex. "I solemnly swear to be the best tour guide in the history of this ballpark. You know what...I'll be the best tour guide in the history of this whole island."

He pulled into his assigned parking space, turned off the car, then hopped out with the same enthusiasm he'd once used when trying to slide into home plate. Dane wanted to make sure he reached the passenger side of the car before Mandy opened her door.

"Thanks," Mandy said as Dane pulled the door wide.

Instinctively, Dane's left hand reached down, and Mandy took it with no hesitation. The touch of her skin on his triggered memories from earlier in the afternoon when she'd come to a dead stop on the jogging trail and shot down the fear that had wrapped him like a blanket—and then offered her support and friendship by simply being there and putting out her hand.

He wanted to tell her thank you for saying all that she had earlier. Unfortunately, a short phrase of gratitude seemed inadequate. Plus, in his heart, he knew wasn't ready to have a conversation with any real depth. Dane was still sorting out his own emotions and what the twists and turns of this week—and especially this day—meant for him.

He didn't know this God that Mandy was talking about. But he felt now like he knew Mandy. And because of that, he gave the words she had spoken with such conviction the benefit of any doubt.

"Come on, let's go inside and I'll show you around."

They walked down the sidewalk in front of the ballpark and past the three windows of the ticket booth. Dane jingled his keys in his hands as they walked up to a glass door at the end of the breezeway, tucked in beside the booth where the souvenirs and T-shirts were sold.

"What on Earth is all that?" Mandy tried to stifle a laugh as she looked at the size of Dane's key ring. "What do you do with all of those?"

"Well, I open a lot of doors. Locker rooms, training rooms, meeting rooms, offices, workout rooms...you name it. If it's a door in this ballpark and you need it open, I'm your guy."

For a split second, Dane wished he was talking about something other than opening the office door. He enjoyed being around Mandy—and he wouldn't mind spending more time with her, getting to know her better, and maybe in the future, being her guy.

"Oooh. So, you're saying you're kind of a big deal?"

She sounded like she was flirting, and he wasn't about to stop her.

"Well yeah," he replied. "I mean, I've even got the key to where the fireworks are."

Mandy put her hands on her hips. "In charge of the fireworks? Now that sounds dangerous...and intriguing."

Dane adjusted the ball cap on his head. "Come to the game and I'll show you what I mean."

Things were warming up in the breezeway, and it had nothing to do with Provident Island's summer heat. It took every ounce of self-control Dane had not to pull her close and set off some sparks right here in front of the souvenir stand.

He'd spent too many years of his life waiting for the perfect pitch to come across the plate. It was an equal blend of adrenaline and power held in check. He loved the feeling of knowing you could go wide-open at any moment, but you had to hold back and learn to watch for the right signs that told you *this* was what you were waiting for.

Dane's days at the plate had been over for a while. But this back-and-forth with the ponytailed professor pumped the same kind of force of will through his veins. He knew he wanted to get to know her better.

She wasn't the first woman who'd intrigued him. But unlike the skirts he'd chased in his days on the road, Dane saw Mandy differently. He'd come to Port Provident to put his past in the past and focus on his future. Dane thought his future had been wrapped up in Cole and the relationship they could build together.

But now there was another relationship he wanted to build as well, one with Mandy McGovern.

"We have fireworks on Friday nights after the game. It's a fun thing to do, and we get good turnout from the community."

"How have I missed this?" The smile hadn't left her face, but the expression in her velvet eyes had narrowed their focus, zeroing in on his face.

"I don't know," Dane said. "But I'll leave a ticket at the will-call window tonight so you can fix the problem. First pitch is at seven-o'-five."

"I'd like that. I'd also still like a quick tour if we still have time."

Baseball had taught him that waiting on the perfect pitch could take time. Dane didn't want to swing and miss. He unlocked the door and held it open.

"I promised you the best tour on the island. Come on inside."

MANDY COULDN'T BELIEVE how much fun this evening had been. It brought back so many childhood memories of running around with friends and eating all the junk food she could.

When she arrived at will-call, she discovered that her reserved seat wasn't actually in the stands with the other fans. Instead, Dane had set aside the end of the bench in the dugout for her. He'd introduced her to the team as the professor who was helping Cole with some of his concussion recovery therapies, and they'd all warmed up to her presence immediately. Several stopped by individually before the game to thank her for assisting their teammate.

Dane had prepared for her comfort during the game almost as meticulously as he'd prepared for the game itself. A bucket next to her designated spot held bottles of soda and water, an overflowing container of popcorn, and four bags of peanuts.

Mandy watched as Dane touched his cap, then his arm, and brushed his wrist twice, signaling to the runner back at second base.

He'd been focused the first time they'd met and he asked for her help. He'd been involved as she explained aspects of TBI and testing and therapies in layman's terms. He'd been engaged as she pushed back on his theories of punishment with the truth of God's love.

But she'd never seen him like this before—totally immersed. It was clear this game was his passion. And she loved watching him live it out. She felt the same kind of pride and joy as she did when a student of hers took what she taught and applied it out in classrooms to make a difference for other kids.

As a teacher, there was often no greater joy than seeing learning absorbed and used and passed on.

As a friend, there was no greater joy than seeing someone right where they belonged, doing what they'd been made to do.

And Dane Vasquez had been made to coach this game and mentor these young men. Whether he cheered them on, made adjustments to the game plan, gave input on technique, or simply gave a high-five after a good play, Mandy found herself more caught up in what Dane was doing than in the game itself.

She shelled another peanut, licking the salt off the husk, then popping the inner morsel in her mouth.

Dane walked by and gave her knee a squeeze as he passed. Something inside Mandy fizzed like the bubbles in the bottle of soda on the ground at her feet.

She loved feeling like a kid again—but even more, she loved feeling like a grown-up woman every time she followed Dane with her eyes.

"Just gotta get Lark home, and then I promised you some fireworks," he said.

Mandy laughed. She'd been feeling aglow already for nine innings.

"What's that about?" He took his eyes off the field for a second and looked back at where Mandy was seated.

She waved it off. "Nothing. Go win the game."

"As you wish." He flashed her his wide grin and gestured at the field with his hand. The batter cracked a shot to the outfield that landed between the shortstop and the center fielder. As it rolled a few yards on the ground, Dane whirled his arm forcefully in a circle, waving Lark around third base and toward home. As Lark approached, he took a dive and slid for the plate, touching the white rubber with his fingertips just seconds before the throw from the field.

The guys next to her on the bench jumped up *en masse*, and Mandy found herself shooting straight up with the same level of excitement. She slapped hands high and low—and she was pretty sure someone slapped her quickly on the backside, though she couldn't tell if it was an accident or on purpose. Maybe it was a dugout rite-of-passage.

Suddenly, a pair of strong arms slipped around her waist and tightened, lifting her off the ground. Her feet kicked slightly as she was spun in a small circle.

Dane leaned his head low and she could smell minty bubblegum as he whispered just above her ear. "We weren't supposed to beat these guys. Their starter tonight is an ace. You're my new good-luck charm."

"It didn't look like you needed any luck. Y'all played with control the entire time. I never would have guessed you thought you were the underdog."

He put Mandy down, and she couldn't help but take notice of the brush of her body against his as she slid down his chest before her feet hit the ground.

"Heeeey, Coach…" Mandy turned her head slightly and saw Lark Thomas, still on a high from scoring the game-winning run in the bottom of the ninth, giving his coach a knowing look.

Within seconds, a cold wave poured down from above. Orange liquid sluiced down her hair, over her shoulders, and fell in a heap at her feet, splashing back up to mid-calf from the force with which it hit the ground.

Mandy sputtered and wiped her eyes with her fingers. She looked over at Dane. Sports drink dripped from the brim of his cap. His uniform no longer matched the school's blue-and-white color palette.

Suddenly, the sound of an oversized cooler hitting the ground broke through the hoots and hollers, and then the laughter of about twenty college-age boys began to reverberate off the metal roof of the dugout and the walls.

"Yeah, you'd better run," Dane shouted back at the perpetrators as they scrambled up the far set of stairs and took off across the field.

Mandy wiped some stray hairs back from her forehead. "So that was a first."

"You don't get power drink showers in Porter Hall?"

"Not unless something's on fire."

Mandy hoped he didn't notice the flush she could feel prickling at her cheeks. He didn't need to know *she* was on fire. But this was something another orange drink dousing wouldn't help. In fact, it made things even more problematic because while no man ever looked bad in baseball pants, Dane Vasquez looked absolutely smoking. Those wet baseball pants made the results of hours in the gym even more visible.

She needed to turn away before she got burned by thinking of Dane Vasquez as more than the parent of a student she was assisting.

"Come on, let's go find some towels." He slipped an arm around her shoulders.

At that touch, Mandy knew she was roasting like a campfire marshmallow. Maybe just for tonight, she could play with a little fire. Dane was a worldly guy. Her idea of a crush was probably child's play, compared to the things he'd seen in his time as a professional athlete. The realization steadied her just a bit. She could indulge her three-alarm fun and probably never set off a single bell in his mind.

DANE LED MANDY THROUGH a labyrinth beneath the stadium. "Stay right here for just a second."

He left her in the hall, then ducked inside the locker room and grabbed a stack of towels. Quickly, he decided to make a quick stop at his locker in the coaches' area. He'd been through a number of post-game sports drink showers in his life, but Mandy probably hadn't.

Besides, it was taking all of his self-control to keep his eyes up on her face and not her soaking wet Provident College T-shirt.

She needed some dry clothes before she drove him crazy.

He pulled a clean shirt out of his locker. It was definitely not her size, but a boxy size XL over her small frame would probably do wonders to settle down his erratic pulse right now.

"Got 'em." He handed Mandy a couple of towels and the T-shirt. "Come this way, you can change in my office."

She tugged on his hand. "No I can't."

Dane gave her a questioning look. "Why not?"

"Because you promised me fireworks. Shouldn't they be starting soon?"

Dane raised his eyebrows, a wordless salute to his big mouth. There were plenty of fireworks in this underground hallway, she just didn't know it. Clearly, she had no idea what the sight of her was doing to him.

He couldn't take her and her wet shirt back to the dugout. There were still too many people milling around and they'd get more of the well-respected professor than they'd bargained for. Dane thought for a minute, then grabbed her hand. "Come on."

They sprinted through the back of the underground area and navigated up three flights of stairs designated only for those working at the ballpark.

"This is where the media and broadcast rooms are." Dane pointed at the metal double doors leading to the third floor. "One more to go."

Dane opened the door at the top of the stairs. "Ok, go out there and step to your right. It's narrow, so be careful."

The moon sparkled out over the water. Beaten down by the summer heat, the waves barely stirred and the surface was almost flat, except for gentle rolls here and there.

"Where are we?" Mandy's voice was breathless.

"This is where the guys come to raise the flags at the top of the ballpark façade." He pointed behind where they were standing, to a set of tall poles.

"It's amazing. You can see the whole campus from here—and all the way down Gulfview Boulevard. She craned her head toward the end of the island. "Wow, you can even see the lighthouse."

Suddenly, a sound like giant popcorn came from the behind the wall of the ballpark.

"And fireworks," said Dane. "You can definitely see the fireworks."

The multi-colored sparks began to fly upward and burst into patterns, but Dane had no interest in them. He only had eyes for Mandy.

"Aren't you going to watch?"

"I've seen them before."

The corner of her mouth snuck upward. "Well, you've seen me before, too."

Dane turned toward her and placed a hand on each of Mandy's shoulders. "Not like this." The golden glow from the fireworks lit her face with sparkles and light.

There was no going back now.

He leaned down and put his lips squarely on top of hers. The controlled explosions weren't just breaking and lighting the sky around them. The fireworks were here, on this parapet, in this first kiss.

She tasted like salty snacks and sugary orange. Dane noted the contrast—so like Mandy. Sweet, yet stubborn. Helpful, yet determined.

Suddenly, he lost himself in the kiss and realized it wasn't a contradiction. It was the sweetest moment in the hottest summer night.

Mandy was home and faith and learning and understanding.

She was everything he'd been looking for, all wrapped up in one. He kept his eyes close, not caring that he was missing the display of light and sparkle all around him.

And when Mandy slid her arm around the back of his neck, his heartbeat pulsed and popped in time with the aerial display. He'd been celebrating victories at ballparks since he was four years old.

But never until now had Dane realized he'd slid home without ever touching the base.

He deepened the kiss, and in doing so, deepened the awareness of the pull Mandy had on his heart. As the fireworks boomed to their crescendo, Dane knew the moment would soon come to an end. Reluctantly, he pulled away and felt the summer sea breeze twist between their still-soaked shirts.

Mandy's arms still lay atop his shoulders. He searched her eyes, seeing the last of the fireworks reflected back at him.

"You did say you had the key to the fireworks," she said, with a soft smile that sent melted fire through his veins all over again.

Chapter Six

MANDY LOOKED WISTFULLY out of the window in her office at the students crossing the campus below. The first summer semester was underway. And yet, for the first time since she'd come to Provident College, none of those students would be hers this term.

The phone rang, cutting into her pity party.

"Mandy McGovern," she said as she answered the line.

"Hey Mandy, it's Dane."

The full introduction was unnecessary. She knew who it was after the first syllable. She'd spent all weekend at the end of the dugout bench, watching the team's games. She'd listened to all his interactions with his players, and with Cole, who came out to support his teammates on Saturday night. Cole also made it halfway through the Sunday afternoon game before the bright sunlight took a toll on his vision and triggered a headache.

And through it all, Dane had been there, offering advice and encouragement—to his kids on the team and to his biological one.

She tried to be nonchalant as she replied back. She knew he'd tease her if he found out how much time she'd spent turning over every moment of the weekend in her mind.

Especially that kiss at the top of the ballpark as the moon shone over the water and fireworks danced in the sky around them.

That kiss had spent a lot of time replaying in her mind and in every nerve and fiber of her body.

"Hi there. What's up?" There. That sounded perfect. Friendly, yet nothing out of the ordinary.

"Cole called this morning on his way to class. He said he brought along the kit of oils you made for him. But he wanted to know if you could meet him at the baseball offices this afternoon instead of at your office."

"Sure, whatever's easiest for him." It wasn't like she had anywhere else to be today.

"I think he wants to hang out with his friends this afternoon. It helps him feel a little less...different...to be able to see them and all, even if he can't go out and take batting practice or anything like that."

"I totally get it." After a weekend around the team and their infectious spirit and support for each other—and their head coach—Mandy thought that it would probably be good medicine for Cole. "What time?"

"He said he'd be here about two." Dane paused a second and mumbled something to someone else. "Sorry, that was my assistant. She needed me to sign something. Anyway, I thought maybe we could have lunch first."

Mandy's heart did a double thump. She'd love nothing more than to see Dane and spend a little more time with him. It would probably be good medicine for her, considering her sad mood as she'd watched the students from afar. But she couldn't go out to lunch today.

She'd thought about one or two other things besides Dane and that kiss this weekend, and one of them was her precarious financial situation. She needed to make it through the next ten weeks on her savings, until she was back on the official full payroll in August. That meant no more lunches in the faculty dining room.

"I'd love to, but I can't." The admission made her more depressed than watching the students had. "No full paycheck this summer means I'm going to be brown-bagging it when I'm up here on campus."

"Perfect."

She hadn't really expected that kind of enthusiasm over penny-penching.

"What do you mean, 'perfect'?"

"I want to go to the Lighthouse. It's a perfect day to go get some sunshine and salt breeze. I'll pick up a sandwich and chips from the cafeteria, then I'll come pick you up about noon. How about that?"

She looked at the sack lunch on the table behind her desk. "My peanut-butter-and-jelly will probably taste better on the beach."

"I can guarantee it."

"You guarantee a lot, Dane Vasquez. First the fireworks, now lunch."

Dane's hearty laugh vibrated through the phone. "I didn't let you down the first time, did I?"

"No," Mandy said, forced to admit the truth. "No, you sure didn't."

THE EARLY SUMMER DAYS fell into a routine as they waited on for Cole's neuropsychological test results to be complied and evaluated. Mandy would tutor students in the morning for extra income. Dane hit the gym at sunrise with his team and then spent the morning watching film and game planning with his assistant coaches. The Provident College Tidal Waves were at the top of the conference standings, and Dane had every intent of keeping it that way so they could get a good seed at the upcoming conference championship tournament.

These first few weeks of the summer had also made Dane more proud of his son than ever before. Cole attended the two classes he needed to re-take in the morning, then stuck to the plan Mandy had outlined for him. She'd changed his diet to a low-carb, high fat diet to lessen inflammation and feed the brain. She organized the supplements the neurologist wanted him to take. Every afternoon, Mandy and Cole spent an hour together, working on focus and study strategies that would help him without over-taxing his brain. She'd even scheduled nap and rest breaks in his day. Cole took to it all without complaint.

"I'm just crossing my fingers that this is helping and that the test results give him some hope." Dane leaned back in the chair behind his desk. Mandy had just popped her head in his office to give him a report after her daily session with Cole in the coaches' conference room at the end of the hall.

Mandy raised her hand and twisted two of her fingers together, then two more. "I don't get it. How does that help anything?"

"Well, I don't know." It was a little silly, now that he watched her mocking him. "But what else am I supposed to do?"

"Maybe something that works." She raised her eyebrows.

"Like what?"

"Have you ever tried prayer, Dane?"

He popped forward in his chair. "Never. Talking out loud to air doesn't seem any more productive than crossing fingers."

She entered the room and walked over to his desk. "Well, that wouldn't. But talking to the God who created the air and everything it surrounds works miracles."

"Mandy, I can't." His throat got a little dry just thinking about trying to fulfill her request. "The minute I opened my mouth, God's gonna know me as the guy who hasn't been inside a church since age ten. If He's all over the universe, He doesn't have time to listen to guys like me. There have to be a million people in line in front of me who are worth his time."

Mandy leaned forward and braced her hands on the desk. Dane could smell the hint of flowers and mint on her wrists. "Remember what I told you on the trail that day? He's your Father and he wants to know what's on your heart as much as you want to know what's on Cole's."

Before he could reply, Randy Tompkins, one of Dane's assistant coaches knocked on the door. "Got a second? Oh, sorry, Dr. McGovern...I didn't see you there."

"That's okay," Mandy said as she straightened up. She gave Dane a brief nod of the head to emphasize the point she'd made. "We were just finishing up. Dane's got some questions he's got to find the answers to, anyway."

She smiled as she walked out of the office, leaving the crisp floral scent behind. Dane breathed it in like an anchor.

"Well, maybe you can answer my questions too, while you're at it, Coach."

Dane frowned. The scent had faded. "Doubt it, Randy. Tell me something...do you pray?"

"Pray?"

"Yeah, like hands folded and eyes closed and all that stuff."

"Well, like that...only in church on Sunday. But sure, I talk to God quietly in my head as I'm going along in my day."

Dane tilted his head. "You just do that? Doesn't that seem crazy to you?"

Randy shrugged. "Well, maybe. But you know, sometimes, God things just aren't meant to be understood. You just have to have faith and take a swing."

THE NEUROPSYCHOLOGIST was running late. Dane sat in a wing-back chair, while Mandy and Cole sat on the couch directly across from a large walnut desk covered in papers. With every minute that ticked off the loud clock on the far wall, Dane felt his jitters multiply. If the doctor didn't hurry up and make an appearance, Dane felt certain he would turn into a human jumping bean.

He looked over at Cole, whose normally tanned skin had fallen several shades lighter. His foot tapped on the floor in an uncoordinated rhythm. It broke Dane's heart to see his son so nervous about today's conversation.

And more than that, it brought home all the years he'd missed with Cole. Dane was fully experiencing the concept of hurting along with your child, but how many times growing up had his son needed him and he hadn't been there?

Thank God Cole'd had a devoted mother and a good stepfather to stand in the gap where Dane had failed to be.

Thank God, indeed. Dane sat up straighter as he realized that he meant those words as an actual expression of thanks.

Thank you, God, for giving my son people in his life that have supported him as he's grown.

Dane let out a breath as he realized he'd done exactly what Randy had described a few days ago—he'd just spoken the words to God in his head, informally. There were no candles, no incense, no perfect bowing postures. Only true words, coming straight from his heart.

And somehow, he knew God heard them. He couldn't say how, but something in his heart told him he'd done the right thing.

The door hinges squeaked, announcing Dr. Post as she stepped in the room.

"Cole, Coach Vasquez. It's good to see you again." She stretched out a hand in greeting. "And Dr. McGovern, how are you today?"

"Doing well," Mandy said. Dane could tell Mandy was just as nervous about today's outcome as he was. Although he hated that she was worried, in a way, it was reassuring to know she cared deeply about Cole and his well-being.

"Wonderful. Have a seat, and let's start going over these test results. Overall, I think Cole has a great chance at recovery. He's young and we know time is one of the best healers for brain injury. That said, there are some things at play from these test results that show me that Cole has most definitely been affected by this injury. I'll go over these more in detail shortly, but Cole does have a narrow window of focus—he begins to tune out at about three minutes. Additionally, he does have some executive function deficits. Basically speaking, when I say executive function, I'm talking about Cole's ability to take in and process information and turn it back around. His memory is stronger than I expected, but his ability to work under deadlines, or make sense of lectures and assignments are impaired."

A wave of crushing sickness coursed through Dane's body. He'd already seen the evidence in Cole's behavior, but to hear it from a professional made it so much more real. "What can we do, Dr. Post?"

"I'd like to recommend that Cole take the rest of the summer completely off. No classes. Rest and neurocognitive therapy only."

From the corner of his eye, Dane saw Mandy making notes in a small spiral-bound notepad.

"What about baseball?" Cole's voice came out small and hushed. "Will I ever get to play again?"

Dr. Post shook her head. "Probably not. You can't risk getting another concussion. Without swift and substantial recovery, I couldn't in good conscience sign any medical clearances to let you play again."

Cole dropped his head in his hands. Immediately, Mandy reached out her arm and pulled him close.

Dane dropped to his knees and scooted over to the couch, reaching his arms up to his son and to Mandy. The three of them held on to each other in place of the hope they'd held onto for these past weeks. He felt his heart blowing away like the sand that lined Port Provident's beaches. When he'd decided to turn his life around, he'd had a dream to bond with his son over baseball.

With just a few words from Dr. Post, that dream was gone.

"Dad?" Cole looked into Dane's eyes. Tears dotted the bottom lid, but had not yet spilled back over. "If it's okay with you, I'd like to go back to Illinois for the summer. I think it'll hurt too much to be here around my friends if I can't do anything with them."

Dane swallowed past the lump in his throat. He couldn't lose his son, not now, not when they were just finding each other. But how could he stand in the way of Cole's wishes?

God give me the strength to do this.

Dane lifted his hand, despite the shaking, and placed it on Cole's knee. "Of course, Cole. And I'll always be waiting for you to come back home. You and I will get our chance to know each other and be father and son."

Chapter Seven

MANDY TOOK CAREFUL footsteps down the hallway in the baseball offices. Her vision was partially blocked by the unwieldy cardboard box she carried out in front of her, and she didn't want to trip.

If she was completely honest with herself, she trusted her feet a lot more than she trusted her heart.

She didn't want to run into Dane. Literally, with the box—or figuratively.

Ever since the meeting with Dr. Post, Dane had changed. Instead of texting her in the middle of the day just to chat, or leaving her special ticket at will-call, he'd gone virtually radio silent. Dealing with his son's future, packing him up to go back to Illinois for the remainder of the summer, and knowing they would never get to achieve their shared baseball dream had taken an instant and very visible toll on Dane.

The last time she talked with him, more than a week ago, he'd said he needed to put his head down and focus on the upcoming conference championship series in Houston.

Mandy had tried to take Dane at his word, but she'd seen him at work earlier in the season. He was completely at-ease with the game, and his coaching style was more instinctive than studied. She knew that the real reason he'd slipped out of her life had nothing to do with his upcoming baseball games, yet had everything to do with baseball.

"Dr. McGovern—can I help you?" Randy Tompkins stepped out of his office as Mandy passed by. "That's a big box. Are you headed out to the parking lot?"

"I am. And some help would be great, but please just call me Mandy."

She decided to take Randy's help not because the box was a strain, but because he'd be able to move more quickly than she could. And the less time she spent in the baseball offices, the less likely she'd be to see Dane.

The less likely she was to see Dane, the more likely she was to not spend the rest of the day replaying every word and looking for meanings that just weren't there.

Randy slipped his arms around the box and started to move down the hallway. "What'cha got here? Do you mind my asking?"

"No, not at all. This is the last of the things Cole and I were using in our study hall we'd set up in the small conference room." She steeled herself not to turn her head and look as she walked past Dane's closed office door. "Have y'all heard from Cole since he's been home?"

Randy turned around and backed slowly into the glass door to open it, "Dane's talked to him a few times. His mom is taking good care of him. He's bored because she's not letting him do anything—not even watch TV—all he gets to do is go to his cognitive rehab appointments. But he did talk Nancy into letting him watch the games when we get to the conference tournament, so he's got something to look forward to. He also said he's keeping up with the therapies you sent him home with. He really likes your diffuser. He said the oils help him sleep better at night."

That made her smile. At least she'd been able to make some kind of difference for him.

"I hope the rest and rehab helps him. He's a great kid with a lot of determination."

Randy held the door open as Mandy passed through. "He is. He gets it from his dad. I've never seen anyone as tough as nails in the pinch as Dane is. He doesn't make a big deal out of it. He just assesses the situation, decides what needs to be done—and *boom!*—does it. He doesn't second-guess much of anything."

Mandy knew Randy's assessment was pretty accurate, but she felt the air go out of her like a deflated balloon at his words. No doubt Dane had decided that being around her was no longer necessary after Cole went back to Illinois. Maybe seeing her was too painful for him. No matter what the reason happened to be, the truth was Dane appeared to have sized up the connection she thought they both felt for each other—and then—*boom!*—put it behind him.

She unlocked her car on the front row of the ballpark parking lot. As she turned to give Randy room to maneuver the box into the back seat of her sedan, a flag waving at the top of the stadium caught her eye.

It fluttered, beckoning her to remember the kiss that happened up there, the evenings at the ballpark, the lunches at the base of the famous Port Provident Lighthouse that ended with more kisses. It called her to remember the fireworks. Not the ones she'd seen with her eyes—although they'd dazzled and sparkled and reflected on the water—but the ones she'd felt in her heart and her veins and that Dane had told her he felt too.

The ocean breeze whipped the fabric of the flag and called to the memories she'd stored inside. But like Dane, it was time to do what needed to be done. Like Cole, she was going to leave campus and take a break from everything this summer. A few weeks away, taking full advantage of no teaching load, would do Mandy some good.

She pulled her gaze down and locked the memories in her heart.

The past was officially in the past.

"DANE! GOT A MINUTE?" Peter Downley, Provident College's Athletic Director, stepped across the red dirt edging the grassy baseball field.

"Sure." Dane strode back toward home plate, a little uncertain about why his boss had come to The Splash in the middle of the day on a Tuesday. Usually he called first. "What's up, Peter?"

"I just got out of a meeting and was thinking about Cole. How's he doing?"

"Talked to him this morning, actually. He said he's been getting a lot of rest and is starting to notice the brain fog lessening. He's got an in-office concussion protocol evaluation Monday at his neurologist's office, and he's hoping for some good news. The doctor said if he sees progress this month and next month, he'll release him to come back to school in the fall and continue his cognitive rehab here."

"But playing baseball is still out?"

Dane nodded. "All of his doctors have made it very clear that ship has sailed. He's not going back on a field. Too much risk."

Peter tucked one hand into a pocket. "I hate that for him—and for you—but I thought that's what was going to happen. That's part of why I stopped by today. I want him to continue his education here at Provident College, and I want to give him the Athletic Director's Choice scholarship. It's a resource we have for students who are not able to continue with our teams because of career-ending injuries. There aren't any grade requirements or time restrictions attached. We'll pay for Cole to finish school as long as it takes. There's no pressure on him. I just want to see him graduate and be set up for success."

Gratitude washed over Dane like the roll of the waves off the Provident Island shore. "That's amazing, Peter. I'll tell him. Thank you. That will be a huge relief for him. I know he wants to earn his degree once the doctors clear him."

"You're welcome, Dane. He deserves it. He's a good kid."

Dane couldn't do anything other than agree. "He's the best—a true fighter."

The two men walked slowly around the perimeter of the field as they talked.

"I've got one other thing I wanted to talk to you about."

Dane felt his jaw twitch just a little bit. Something about the way his boss said that particular phrase made him a little nervous. "I heard Mandy McGovern from the Education

Department worked with Cole for a few weeks before he left. Can you tell me what she was doing?"

Peter was known around the conference and in collegiate sports overall as a shrewd negotiator who kept his cards to the vest. It was how he'd been able to weather the damage of Hurricane Hope and quickly restore and rebuild the athletic programs he was responsible for back to championship caliber.

Dane tried to evaluate the tone in his voice and figure out where Peter was going with the question before he gave an answer, but he couldn't come to a decision.

"She teaches the next generation of educators how to best work with children who have barriers to focus and behavior, like ADHD or autism or other conditions."

In a flash, he sailed back in time to the faculty dining room on the first day he met Mandy. He repeated her own description of her job word-for-word back to Peter.

But that wasn't all he remembered. In his mind's eye, he could see the shallow dimple in her smile as she tried to help him that day. He remembered the jogging trail and the touch of her hand as she straightened out his ideas on God and why Cole remained injured. He remembered promising her a fireworks display and scooping her up, tasting the stickiness of the orange sports drink on her lips.

A chill landed on his shoulders, oblivious to the almost triple-digit temperatures on the field.

He remembered how he'd gone out of his way to wrap himself in his grief over losing Cole's presence in his life and how he pushed Mandy aside too—because she reminded Dane of how he'd tried to help Cole, but instead had been too little, too late once again.

"Do you feel like she made a difference for Cole?"

Dane answered honestly. "I do. She's got some good ideas. She taught him how to use some low-intervention practices to give him more focus and some study skills that I think will serve him well in the future. Mandy was supposed to be on a research sabbatical this summer to learn more about some of these methods, but the funding got cancelled at the last minute. It was actually a blessing for us because she was able to pour all her knowledge into Cole and to help us navigate the tests and therapies."

Peter stopped at first base. "Good to know. I've had some people asking about it."

Dane's eyes opened wide. "Is Mandy in trouble?"

"Not really, no." Peter put his other hand in his other pocket. "Dorothy Patterson at the Success Center was wondering why you didn't come to them."

"He didn't need tutoring. He needed something cutting-edge." Dane knew he'd gone out on a limb to get Mandy's help—and he'd do it again. And he would fight anyone who tried to cause a problem for Mandy simply because she gave help to someone in need.

"And you think these ideas of Dr. McGovern's worked?"

"Cole is still using many of them now, even though he's not here in school. They've worked a lot of her ideas into his cognitive rehab back in Illinois." Dane could feel his blood pressure rising. He wanted to defend Mandy, but putting up too vigorous of a challenge would cause his very astute boss to start asking other questions—questions Dane absolutely didn't want to answer.

Dane knew if he had to answer them for Peter, he'd have to answer them for himself as well.

"Good to know," Peter said succinctly. "That helps me out a bit. I'll see you at the Athletic Department Awards Dinner, right?"

Once a year, Peter's entire staff gathered to recognize the hard work of all the professionals who supported, coached, and managed the athletes and the game operations. This year, the timing wasn't ideal for Dane, with the conference championship tournament beginning the following week, but he knew missing the event would be a career-limiting move.

"Absolutely."

"Good," Peter said with a quick smile and a nod. "I'll see you there. I'll have Lacey put your seat right up front."

"Ha. Thanks, boss."

Peter gave a wave as he walked off the field, leaving Dane standing near the base line with too many questions. He was going to need to start making some phone calls and so he could find out what this was and to fix it for Mandy if he could.

Dane needed to talk through his feelings about his conversation just now with Peter, about his fear that he might have dragged Mandy afoul of rules that the Success Center had for student-athletes. He knew crossing his fingers and hoping for the best wasn't going to work here. Had his pride and all-consuming need to get the status quo returned in his son's life and his own caused issues for Mandy?

But he was all alone. There was no one to get a sanity check from.

He looked up at the blue sky stretched overhead and dotted with puffy white clouds making their way out to shade the waves of the Gulf of Mexico. He'd have to try things Randy's way.

A tug at his heart reminded him it was Mandy's way too.

I've messed up so many times. Please don't let me have messed up things for her, as well. Help me make this right.

He pulled his cell phone out of his back pocket and dialed the number to Dorothy's office at the Success Center.

MANDY TURNED OVER THE formal card stock in her hand. Someone had written her name on the envelope in fancy black calligraphy, but she couldn't figure out why on earth she'd been invited to the Athletic Director's staff awards night.

She'd RSVP'd "yes" for one reason and one reason only. They'd included a card for meal selection and asked her to indicate her preference. Mandy chose steak.

She was tired of brown bags and peanut butter and jelly sandwiches. The summer of economizing was starting to bore her palate. The invitation said the event began at seven o'clock in the evening. Mandy glanced at the time display on her phone. Six-fifty-eight.

Her goal was to sneak in, sit at the back by the door, eat steak, and avoid Dane.

She opened the door to the banquet room in the student life building, where the event was to be held. Lark Thomas stood in his uniform.

"Good evening, Dr. McGovern," he said, formally.

She eyed him sideways. "Good evening, Mr. Thomas. You've never once called me Dr. McGovern, and you know it."

"True. But I'm an usher this evening. The AD said we had to use our best manners." He put out his hand. "May I show you to your table?"

As long as it's at the back of the room, she thought to herself. "By all means."

Quickly, Mandy realized she was not going to get her wish. Instead, Lark guided her through the sea of tables, and stopped at a chair at the very first table in front of the speaker's podium. He pulled out the empty seat.

Mandy nodded and thanked Lark and went to sit down, then noticed the place card next to her.

Dane Vasquez, Head Baseball Coach

Her heart sunk to the bottom of her strappy summer sandals. She should have just eaten another PB&J. This free meal came with far too high of a price.

"Coach, hey!" Lark's voice boomed just behind Mandy's head. "I mean...it's very nice to see you here this evening, Coach Vasquez."

Dane laughed, and it pierced straight to the center of Mandy's heart. She'd missed that slightly sarcastic sound lately. She hadn't even realized how much until just now.

"Cut the choirboy act, Thomas."

"Yes, sir. Enjoy your evening."

Mandy stared straight ahead as she heard Dane pull out the chair next to her. Her breathing sped up and she could feel the breaths stopping far short of her diaphragm. Their lack of cooperation made her light-headed. She could not look to her right. Dane could not know he had this kind of effect on her.

He'd forgotten about her. She needed to at least pretend like she'd forgotten about him.

"I...um...I don't think I've ever seen you with your hair down before, Mandy."

Well, if that wasn't the strangest greeting ever, Mandy didn't know what was. Why was he stammering? And why did he choose to comment on her hair? Self-consciously, she smoothed it behind her ears, wishing she'd just pulled it back in her trusty ponytail.

"It seemed like we were supposed to dress up." She lost all will-power and snuck a glance to the side. "You're wearing a suit."

As much as she'd enjoyed seeing him in his athletic shorts and baseball pants, Mandy couldn't believe how sharp Dane looked in his crisp black suit with a blue tie that matched the Tidal Waves' official colors.

Now she knew she'd have to focus on the floral arrangement in front of her all evening. Looking to the right was a definite recipe for trouble.

"Speaking of recipes, this had better be the best steak ever," she muttered under her breath.

"What?"

"Nothing." *Absolutely nothing.* Just like what she meant to him.

Thankfully, waiters began passing baskets of bread around the room. When one landed in front of Mandy, she swiped a fluffy wheat roll. As she placed it on her plate, she wondered if she could just stuff the whole thing in her mouth at once so she didn't have to utter any more pleasantries in Dane's direction.

She remembered Lark's admonition that this was a formal event, though, and she was forced to reconsider.

"Mandy, about tonight..." Dane started a sentence, but Mandy waved him off.

"*Sssh*," she said, flapping her hand slightly. "The program is about to start. It's fine. Whatever."

That seemed to sum up anything and everything she wanted to say anyway. Whatever.

The Athletic Director himself emceed the event, dropping in funny anecdotes and touching human interest stories along the way as he highlighted each sport and presented a number of awards. Despite Dane's awkward presence next to her, Mandy allowed herself to enjoy celebrating the many successes of the student-athletes at Provident College and those who coached and worked with them. A few staff award recipients had served with Mandy on the Judicial Affairs council or were in the Faculty and Staff Bible study with her, and Mandy cheered enthusiastically for each award recipient she knew personally.

"This evening isn't just about current success," Peter Downley said into the microphone. "It is about setting a standard, blazing a trail, and doing things that pave the way for future success. One of those areas we've been committed to doing more in is the area of student-athlete health. Many of our students find themselves injured while playing, and I don't have to tell you that concussions are one of the most challenging aspects of athlete health today. We know more than ever before, and we know a full and supported recovery is vital—not just so our athletes can return to the field, but so they can return to the classroom. We want them to be prepared for their future, no matter what that may be."

Mandy's spine straightened. The Athletic Director was speaking her language. She tuned in, keenly interested in whatever he was about to introduce.

"And so because of that, I'd like to present our Trailblazer Award this year to someone who is not actually in our department, but to someone who jumped in to assist one of our student-athletes when he needed it the most. She worked outside the box and the reports I've received show me that there's a lot more coordination we can do between our department and our colleagues on campus. Dr. Mandy McGovern is joining us tonight from the Education Department, and I hope you will all join me in thanking her for the work she did this summer to help Cole Vasquez on the baseball team with his rehabilitation from a severe concussion. Cole's doctors informed him just this afternoon that they're seeing improvements and hope to clear him to come back to PC in the fall. His playing days are over, but his school days are not. Cole will now be here on an academic scholarship, and he'll be joining his dad in the dugout as a team assistant instead of playing. Dr. McGovern, will you please come up here and accept this award with my thanks?"

Mandy stood up and tears began to slip down her cheeks. She picked up her napkin and dotted the corners of her eyes. She'd been shocked to hear her name called, but hearing Cole's progress report lit up her heart and released a flood of emotions.

Just as with any of her students, it wasn't about her. It was about them, their futures, and the lives they would touch. To know that Cole's future was as bright as the fireworks over The Splash—it almost brought her to her knees.

"Coach Vasquez, will you come up with Dr. McGovern?" the AD asked. "I know this is an area near your heart as well, so I'd like for you to share with Dr. McGovern and the rest of your coaching colleagues what's coming next."

Mandy could barely feel her feet as she walked around the front row of tables to get up to where Peter Downley stood. As she rounded the last corner, she felt a palm in the small of her back, steadying her. She closed her eyes just for a moment, and wiped away another tear.

This one wasn't for Cole.

It was for her. It was for Dane, and everything she knew she wanted but could never have.

As she got close to the podium, Peter Downley handed her a certificate in an oversized dark wood frame.

"Thank you," she said. "This means so very much to me. I didn't do it to be recognized. When I learned about Cole's story, I just wanted to help."

The AD held the microphone up again and spoke into it. "The good news is, you're going to have the opportunity to do much more of that. Thanks to a generous gift from Neil and Erica Patton, the lead donors on our success center, we are partnering with the School of Education and Provident Medical Center to create a research lab into concussion rehabilitation for student-athletes, with an emphasis on their academic needs."

He handed the microphone to Dane.

"We want to you to be able to do your research here at Provident College. We want to lead the way in this area," Dane said. "And I want you to know that you were right. Sometimes you're brought to a certain place and certain people for no reason other than it's meant to be."

The crowd stood and began to applaud.

Dane put the microphone back on the stand, then leaned over and wrapped his arms around Mandy, pulling her close. He whispered in her ear. "It's a God thing. I know I some have relationship building to do. With Him, with my son...and with the woman who taught me all of these lessons. I'm sorry I checked out after Cole left, but I know the day you came into my life was definitely a God thing. Can I have another chance? Can we restore what we were in the process of building?"

Mandy leaned further into the embrace. She wanted to reciprocate, but the big frame in her hand prevented her from doing so.

"Can you promise me there will be fireworks?" Thick emotions in her throat kept her from saying more.

"Oh, Mandy. There will always be fireworks."

You Don't Have to Leave Port Provident!

Start Falling for Her First Love Now!

MEG MCMAHON'S SHORT-lived Cinderella story with Dan Clark ended ten years ago. Now he's the head football coach at Port Provident High School and she's determined to stay off his radar while she's back in her hometown for a few weeks in order to fulfill an obligation. He bought the lies of the world and put his potential in the NFL above their young marriage, and Meg has never forgiven him—or told him her secret that would change everything. When one chance meeting in the school hallway puts them in each other's path, will Meg hold on to her determination not to put herself in a position to repeat the mistakes of past...or will she turn toward the future and a forever homecoming for the family they'd tried to create so long ago?

If you love quick, sweet escape romance stories filled with hope, heart, and happily-ever-after that will make you swoon and leave you with a smile, you will want to celebrate the holidays with the residents of the beachside small town of Port Provident.

https://books2read.com/FirstKissFireworksBook[1]

Join Kristen's Reader Community Today and Receive a Free Port Provident Story

---

1. https://books2read.com/FallingForHerFirstLoveBook

Join Kristen's reader community today for the latest and get A Place to Find Love, a sweet escape romance that introduces you to Port Provident, Texas and the residents who find love on the island, for free!
*www.kristenethridge.com/newsletter*²

Sneak Peek: Falling for Her First Love—Chapter One

NOTHING LOOKED OUT of place. Even the slightly worn Columbia-blue-and-white linoleum tiles covering the hallway of Port Provident High School didn't appear any different than when Meg McMahon last stepped down the corridor.

More than ten years had flown off the calendar, but less than a week back in town made Meg feel as though she'd walked back into a time warp. To the untrained eye, time had not moved on. But Meg knew that to be a lie. She'd last walked down this hall on her graduation day. Just a few hours later, she'd gotten married in a whirlwind trip to the justice of the peace one county over. Port Provident's favored son, the star, the all-state quarterback, Dan Clark, had turned a child from a badly-broken home into a fairy tale princess. He'd taken her from the ashes and made her Cinderella.

But everyone knew fairy tales weren't real. And apparently, neither was Dan Clark's love.

Meg tried to focus on the mission at hand and keep the memories at bay. She just needed to bring Lamont's medical clearance form to the trainer. As she stepped out of the main high school building and walked down the back sidewalk at the edge of the student parking lot, she formulated a plan.

She would just duck inside the field house and lay the single sheet of paper on the trainer's desk. Thinking back to the layout of this building,

Meg knew it wouldn't be hard to run in and run out—assuming that, like the high school itself, the field house probably hadn't changed much either. In those years when she was Dan Clark's one-and-only, Meg had often been by his side while he got his ankle taped or got checked after practice. She knew right where the trainer's room was. She wouldn't need to get anywhere near the field where her ex-husband —now the head football coach at Port Provident High School—was conducting a practice for this week's season-opening game.

Meg pulled open the heavy metal door on the side of the squat, windowless building. Olfactory memory jumped front and center. She knew this smell. Most people would write it off as sweat and gym socks. Instead, Meg remembered hard work, dedication, and dreams. She'd never stepped on a field, but they'd been her dreams too. Her dreams for her future with Dan had been all wrapped up in football.

"Can I help you?"

Meg stopped, but couldn't turn to face the man who called to her.

Even her toes curled under with the instant recognition.

It was the boy her mama had warned her about.

Well, Trudy had technically been her aunt and the boy was now a man. But, as Trudy predicted more than a decade ago, Dan had ultimately broken Meg's heart.

And as that poor, wounded heart pounded in her chest, Meg knew she wasn't as over the events as she'd hoped.

She knew she should turn around. She knew she should reply to the well-intentioned question. But she couldn't.

The sound of footsteps on the concrete floor came closer.

And then it happened. Two fingers lightly tapped her on the shoulder. The touch she'd dreamed about for almost ten years.

Meg sighed slightly, wishing that the casual graze across the top of her T-shirt sleeve meant the security it had once signaled to her. Not this heart-thumping, sticky-sweating, feeling of fear and anxiety.

Slowly, she turned and looked into the eyes of her past.

"Meg?" Dan's whisper echoed in the stark hallway. "What are you doing here?"

"This." She stuck Lamont's form out and took one step back, not trusting herself to be close enough to touch or to speak more than a single syllable. He wouldn't reach out again, she knew—he never had—not even once—since he cut her out of his life.

She also didn't trust herself not to slap him silly. One open-palmed paddle across the cheek for every sleepless night she'd had since leaving the cramped collegiate apartment they'd called their own.

Dan took the page from her outstretched hand, grabbing the corner diagonally across from where Meg's hand held on. She felt thankful for the distance. Even eight-and-a-half-by-eleven inches of paper seemed like protection right now. She would take what she could get.

"Lamont Brown's medical clearance? Why do you have this?" Dan's head cocked at a slight angle.

"He's staying with Trudy." She wanted to keep things as simple as possible right now. They'd been complicated enough for so long.

Dan nodded, still fixing her with that pinching stare. "I know that. Are you staying with Trudy?"

Meg released her hold on the paper and watched the corner float downward. She didn't want to look Dan in the eye anymore. The weight of his stare continued to push on her. "Yes."

"After all this time? Why? I know she's asked you before to come...home." He lingered on that last word. Maybe he remembered telling her that he'd be her forever home as he slipped the chip-sized diamond engagement ring on her finger after the homecoming football game.

"She wasn't recovering well from her knee surgery and she's got a few big catering jobs in the next few weeks. She needed help. I couldn't say no."

Losing her job last week made it convenient to say yes to Trudy's most recent request to return to Port Provident. Nothing made it easy.

And the reason why stood right in front of Meg.

"Are you staying long?"

Meg wondered why he asked. "Why? Do you need to calculate how long to avoid me? You've been practicing that for a while. You didn't even tell me you were leaving. Just wrote a letter telling me they said you needed to cut some ties." No matter what, at least she knew she wouldn't cry in front of Dan. She'd let go of her last tear for him before she even turned twenty.

All subsequent tears had rained solely for herself.

Or so she'd thought.

"Coach! You coming?" A ray of sunlight cut through the dimness in the corridor as the heavy door to the field opened. A kid, dressed for practice in full pads, stood in the doorway. "Coach Brumley said he needs to ask you something about the drills."

"Yeah, Reese. I'm comin'." Dan ran an open palm down the side of his face and wiped his chin. Meg knew it would feel faintly of five o'clock shadow even though it was barely three in the afternoon.

She'd known everything about him, before...

Watching his simple gesture got the best of her resolve. Memories prickled across her fingertips, drawing the mental memory of a sandpaper rasp beneath them. Meg wedged her hand into the tight jeans pocket just below her hip, trying to erase the feeling with the rub of denim.

"Can you just see that the trainer gets that?" She inclined her head toward the paper in Dan's hand. "Trudy said it was important for Lamont."

His dark hazel eyes were distant—not intent like they had been only moments before. Part of her wanted to know what he was thinking. The other part reminded her that what she didn't know couldn't really hurt her.

"Yeah, he needs this to be able to play this season." Dan turned to walk outside, then stopped abruptly. "Will you be there?"

Once upon a time, she'd always been there for Dan. Because he'd always been there for her. But then, one day, he left.

She stood there without answering until Reese shouted again. "Coach?"

His breath released and the muscle at the back of his jaw locked into place. He pulled his gaze back and caught Meg's glance with a determination that she hadn't seen since that last state playoff game.

"Yeah, Reese. I'm comin'," he said.

And then, once again, Dan Clark walked away without another word.

AS SOON AS DAN STEPPED onto the sidelines of the Port Provident High School football practice field, twenty different voices called at least as many different questions in his direction.

But all he could hear was the silence where Meg's answer to his question should have been. He should have known Meg wouldn't want anything to do with him or Port Provident football. She said she came back to town as a favor to Trudy. She dropped off the medical form as a favor to Lamont.

Meg didn't owe Dan any favors. That much he knew. Not after the way he treated her. He'd asked God for forgiveness for his actions, but he'd never been brave enough to ask Meg.

He didn't deserve her forgiveness.

"Dan? You look like you've seen a ghost." Zack Brumley rapped his best friend on the arm with the clipboard he faithfully carried.

Dan stood, arms crossed, watching the players start their drills. "Meg's back."

A whistle tweeted at the other end of the field.

"Meg McMahon?"

Dan's head whipped around involuntarily. "Clark." He spit out the correction, but he didn't know why it mattered to him.

Zack watched one of his linemen make a tackle. "Not like that, son. Get your head up and look at what you hit. Otherwise, that's a good way to wind up on a stretcher."

His fellow coach never took his eyes off the field. "You've got about as much sense as that boy out there."

"Hmph." Dan knew Zack was right, but he didn't really feel like admitting it.

"You think she kept your last name after everything?" Zack kept watching practice, attempting disinterest.

"I've got to go give Lamont Brown's release to Mitch." Dan needed to get away from Zack's laconic correctness.

Dan tried to watch what was happening on the field as he walked to the far end of the sideline where Mitch Sullivan, the head trainer for the Port Provident Pirates, stood. But he couldn't. All he could think about was running into Meg.

Here.

In Port Provident.

At the field house.

He wondered where she'd been all this time. It didn't take long for him to realize the hangers-on of the Lone Star University football program had filled his head with bad advice. But for Meg's sake, he never tried to find her. She'd deserved to rebuild her life without a fool like him.

And from what he saw today, she'd been doing well. She still had that same petite frame with curves in all the right places and her auburn hair framed her face in a long, wavy style he'd seen on one of those "America's Sweetheart"-type of actresses in a recent movie.

He remembered back to a time when Meg had been his sweetheart. Her shy presence gave him confidence when a hundred people across the country wanted something from him. As a highly-recruited quarterback, the list of collegiate coaches who wanted him to listen to the virtues of their programs seemed to never end. And right behind them came the line of people who wanted something of Dan's success for themselves.

But not Meg. She didn't like the spotlight. She never asked Dan for anything he couldn't give.

And true to form, once again he saw her quietly standing at the edge of the chain link fence, studying the practice field. It looked like she'd never left, like time hadn't passed since she last watched him prowl the lines on this grass. She met his gaze, then scurried off like a spooked deer on the side of one of the sleepy Texas Hill Country highways that wrapped around Lone Star University—where their dreams had both come together and diverged almost simultaneously.

Dan stopped and watched her. He didn't know what the emotion was rising in his chest. Was he glad to see Meg again, or would he—like she predicted—avoid her until she left town?

He needed a game plan. Dan looked at the clipboard in his hand, marked up with Xs and Os. He knew all about game plans. He'd taken this football team to the state semi-finals last year on the strength of his strategies.

As he watched his ex-wife climb in a compact, four-door Mazda at the edge of the parking lot, Dan Clark drew up another quick plan: he would not fumble her heart again. And that meant he had to give her a wide berth while she was in town.

He scanned the sideline again and headed back in Mitch's direction. Focus on the game, Clark. She'll be gone soon enough. Just keep staying out of her way until then.

"DID YOU GET LAMONT'S form turned in?" Trudy called from her swing on the front porch.

Meg stuffed her keys in the small pocket at the back of her purse as she walked up the steps to the Victorian house in the heart of Port Provident.

"Yes, it's taken care of." She wished she could say the same about her heart. It hadn't slowed down since she first heard Dan's voice in the field house hallway.

Trudy pointed at the white wicker chair next to the swing. "Have a seat. You've been running every minute since you got back to Port Provident."

Sinking into the tufted red-and-white striped cushion atop the chair, Meg finally relaxed a bit. It felt good to be cradled in something soft. "There's just lots to do before the Bassett anniversary dinner tonight."

"I know, but it'll all get finished." Trudy patted Meg's hand. "I'm sorry that chain bought out the hotel you worked for and reorganized you out of a job. But on the other hand, I'm so glad it happened and gave you the opportunity to come back home. I've missed getting to see you the last few years. You worked so many hours, I didn't get to spend much time with you on my trips to Austin. And I know your culinary skills will be a treat for my clients."

"Mmm-hmm." Meg barely noticed the touch of Trudy's hand.

"You saw him, didn't you?"

"Huh?" Meg turned to look at Trudy. "Who?"

"Dan Clark. You ran into him up at school, didn't you?" Her great-aunt Trudy had been the only real mother Meg had ever known, and her instincts still worked even now that Meg had been an independent adult for years. "I hoped that since practice time had already started, he'd be otherwise occupied."

"He was leaving the field house just as I walked in." Meg wanted to tell Trudy about how her heart raced at the sight of Dan, but she knew she couldn't. Back in the days when everyone said girl with an unstable childhood would be a bad influence on the high school superstar, only Trudy spoke differently. Only Trudy said it would be the other way around.

Trudy said Dan Clark would break Meg's heart.

The events of a decade ago showed Trudy's hunch to be a good one. How could Meg tell her now that as shocking as seeing Dan had been, something deep inside had fluttered with the same excitement she'd felt when she was naïve and eighteen?

For once, she couldn't come clean to Trudy.

"Well, I'll be back on my feet soon, and you'll head back to Austin to look for a new job. With everything going on here between the weddings and the gala at Provident College, it shouldn't be too hard to stay out of his way for a couple of weeks." Trudy leaned forward and sat her empty glass on the small end table that stood just off the edge of the swing. "Can you hand me those crutches, dear?"

Guilt crept up and nudged Meg as she handed the crutches to Trudy. She'd always been able to tell Trudy anything because she knew her great-aunt would unfailingly keep her confidences. Trudy knew the one secret the rest of Port Provident did not. And whether or not Trudy agreed with Meg's reasoning to keep it hush-hush for the last ten years, she never breathed a word. Not at her sewing circle, not at her Bible study, and not in her afternoons when she used to wait tables at Porter's Seafood along Gulfview Boulevard.

Trudy was more than just the mother figure in Meg's life. She was the one person who'd never let her down.

"Will you head upstairs and double check that I pulled out the right table linens for tonight? Oh, and I hate to ask this, but can you straighten up Lamont's room a bit? It smells a bit like teenage boy and sneakers when you get to the top of the stairs." Trudy's crutches made clicking noises with every small step she took. "I'll limp around the kitchen a bit and double check that all the dishes are ready to go in an hour."

At first glance, Lamont's room, off the back of the upstairs landing, looked like a good space for a teenager to call his own. A quilt featuring a navy-and-Columbia blue pirate silhouette on a white background covered the bed. A few pillows in complimentary colors leaned back and obscured most of the headboard. A small student desk with a few drawers and an older wooden chair took up residence under the window at the back of the room. Some papers were scattered across the top. A pair of tennis shoes sat at the end of the bed and a solitary gray T-shirt streaked with sweat stains was tossed carelessly over the top of another chair near the closet.

Nothing seemed out of the ordinary. But Meg could see something was missing. Something important. Personal possessions.

No snapshots in frames lined the bookshelf, no collectibles sat out with pride, no piles of a teenage wardrobe casually heaped in the corner. Not even a well-worn stuffed animal saved throughout the years could be seen.

Foster kids didn't bring much with them from home to home.

Just their hopes for the future. And often times, there wasn't even enough of that to bring along.

Meg remembered the day when she came to Trudy's house after the death of her grandmother. After Meg left, Trudy declared the house too quiet and went through formal certification to be a foster parent. Ten years of children had been loved since then.

She couldn't see much to tidy up, as Trudy asked—Lamont had even made his bed before heading to school this morning—so Meg attacked the few items in plain sight. She plucked the shirt off the chair back and placed it in the hamper, and moved the shoes inside the closet.

Meg stopped at the desk and started to organize the scattered papers into a neat pile. Picking up the white sheets, she couldn't help but notice a bright yellow sticky note affixed to a page of recent math homework. Hastily scribbled on the small square was a name and phone number which began with the Austin area code.

Barry Haynes.

Liquid electricity surged through her veins. In one swift motion, she peeled the sticky note off the other page. Errant corners poked into her palm as she crushed the note in her hand.

Meg hadn't officially met Lamont Brown yet. But she knew there was no way she was going to let slick-talking Barry Haynes ruin one more vulnerable kid's life. He'd already come dangerously close to ruining hers a long time ago. At one time, she'd been paralyzed by the fear Barry put in her. She'd just done what she'd been told and kept quiet. He told her it would be better for her that way. She'd recognized the threat when she heard it.

Meg grabbed her keys and took off running for her car.

Keep reading First Kiss Fireworks

Click here: https://books2read.com/FallingForHerFirstLoveBook

The Holiday Hearts Series

The Right Resolution[3]
The Cupid Caper[4]
Lucky in Love[5]
May I Have This Dance[6]
First Kiss Fireworks[7]
Falling For Her First Love[8]
Thankful for Love[9]
Mission: Mistletoe[10]

Want to extend your stay in Port Provident?
Start reading the Hearts and Hope Series
Shelter from the Storm[11]
The Doctor's Unexpected Family[12]
His Texas Princess[13]
Holiday of Hope[14]
Other Books by Kristen

---

3. http://www.books2read.com/TheRightResolutionBook

4. http://www.books2read.com/TheCupidCaperBook

5. http://www.books2read.com/LuckyInLoveBook

6. http://www.books2read.com/MayIHaveThisDanceBook

7. http://www.books2read.com/FirstKissFireworksBook

8. https://books2read.com/FallingForHerFirstLoveBook

9. http://www.books2read.com/ThankfulForLoveBook

10. http://www.books2read.com/MissionMistletoeBook

11. http://www.books2read.com/ShelterFromTheStorm

12. http://www.books2read.com/TheDoctorsUnexpectedFamily

13. http://www.books2read.com/HisTexasPrincess

14. http://www.books2read.com/HolidayOfHope

Love Hallmark movies? Pick up Kristen's book October Kiss, based on the Hallmark movie viewers love! Available anywhere books are sold—in paperback, digital, and audio!

October Kiss from Hallmark Publishing[15]

ABOUT KRISTEN

Kristen Ethridge writes Sweet Escape Romance—stories with hope, heart and happily-ever-after—for Harlequin's Love Inspired line, Hallmark Publishing, and Laurel Lock Publishing. She's a Romance Writers of America Golden Heart Award nominee and both a Christian Fiction and Inspirational Romance #1 Best-Selling Author.

You can find Kristen in her native habitat—a Texas patio—where she's likely to be savoring the joy of a crispy taco, along with a glass of iced tea. Scents from her essential oil diffuser are also a must, since she's a certified aromatherapist. She's almost convinced her family that it's normal to talk to imaginary people, as long it goes in a book.

Find her online at http://www.kristenethridge.com where you can get a free story for signing up for her newsletter. You can also follow her adventures in writing at www.facebook.com/kristenethridgebooks[16].

Keep up with Kristen by joining her newsletter list[17] and her author pages on Bookbub[18] and Facebook[19]. If you can't get enough of Port

15. https://www.books2read.com/OctoberKiss

16.   http://www.facebook.com/kristenethridgebooks

17.   http://www.kristenethridge.com/newsletter

18.   https://www.bookbub.com/authors/kristen-ethridge

Provident, come join the Port Provident Community Center[23] on Facebook, the official gathering place for Kristen and her fans.

www.kristenethridge.com[21]

Facebook[22] Instagram[23]

The Port Provident Community[24] Center

Don't forget...if you love sweet escape romances, join Kristen's newsletter[25]!

ACKNOWLEDGEMENTS

Thank you to Dr. Cantrell, Dr. Wilkofsky, Dr. Paulman, and especially Dr. Gonyeau for everything you've done for me this past year. And to Brian and the kids—it's been a heck of a walk through the valley, but I believe we will be ready to climb the mountain again soon.

---

19.   http://www.facebook.com/kristenethridgebooks

20.   https://www.facebook.com/groups/2422381554654795

21. http://www.kristenethridge.com

22. https://www.facebook.com/KristenEthridgeBooks

23. https://instagram.com/kristenethridge

24. https://www.facebook.com/groups/2422381554654795

25. http://www.kristenethridge.com

"Yes indeed, it won't be long now." God's Decree. "Things are going to happen so fast your head will swim, one thing fast on the heels of the other. You won't be able to keep up. Everything will be happening at once—and everywhere you look, blessings! Blessings like wine pouring off the mountains and hills. I'll make everything right again for my people Israel:

'THEY'LL REBUILD THEIR ruined cities.

They'll plant vineyards and drink good wine.

They'll work their gardens and eat fresh vegetables.

And I'll plant *them,* plant them on their own land.

They'll never again be uprooted from the land I've given them."

God, your God, says so.'"

-AMOS 9:14-15 (MSG)

LAUREL LOCK PUBLISHING

Publisher's Note: This is a work of fiction. Names, characters, places, and incidents are a product of the author's imagination. Locales and public names are sometimes used for atmospheric purposes. Any resemblance to actual people, living or dead, or to businesses, companies, events, institutions, or locales is completely coincidental.

Scriptures taken from the Holy Bible, New International Version®, NIV®. Copyright © 1973, 1978, 1984, 2011 by Biblica, Inc.™ Used by permission of Zondervan. All rights reserved worldwide. www.zondervan.com[1] The "NIV" and "New International Version" are trademarks registered in the United States Patent and Trademark Office by Biblica, Inc.™

Book Layout ©2013 BookDesignTemplates.com

---

1.   http://www.zondervan.com/